"Don't be a fool. Come back here!"

Joanne glanced up desperately as Ben called down from the yacht. Then she was over the side into the water before he had a foot on the ladder. She heard him shouting after her. "You'll never make it, Joanne...we're miles from shore!"

It took him some time to start the boat. She heard it coming after her and swam as hard as she could. Ben circled her, the throttle closing, and came up beside her to drag her into the boat.

She dived down and shot up again some way away, her head exploding with the pain of holding her breath. "You silly fool," Ben yelled at her, returning in a circle once more. "You'll drown!"

She was a good swimmer but Joanne knew her chances of reaching the beach were slim. But better to drown than let him do as he planned.

Other titles by

CHARLOTTE LAMB
IN HARLEQUIN PRESENTS

Other titles by

CHARLOTTE LAMB
IN HARLEQUIN ROMANCES

Many of these titles, and other titles in the Harlequin
Romance series, are available at your local
bookseller. For a free catalogue listing all available
Harlequin Presents and Harlequin Romances, send
your name and address to:

HARLEQUIN READER SERVICE,
M.P.O. Box 707,
Niagara Falls, N.Y. 14302

Canadian address:
Stratford, Ontario, Canada N5A 6W2

CHARLOTTE LAMB

twist of fate

Harlequin Books

TORONTO·LONDON·NEW YORK·AMSTERDAM
SYDNEY·HAMBURG·PARIS·STOCKHOLM

Harlequin Presents edition published May 1980
ISBN 0-373-10358-1

Original Hardcover edition published in 1979
by Mills & Boon Limited

CHAPTER ONE

HE stood in the doorway for a moment, his dark eyes moving with indifference around the room, an expression of cold boredom undisguised on his face, ignoring the quick glances and curiosity of his fellow guests.

'Who is he?' Joanne heard the whispered question from a group of guests close to her, and turned her head to stare at him. She had never seen him before, and she was sure she would have remembered if she ever had; he was not the sort of man one forgot. Self-assurance tinted every flicker of thought on his face, every movement of the hard lean body. She was certain he was not an actor, and that was strange in these surroundings. Not even a bad actor, she told herself, and there were plenty of those at Clea's parties. She had cornered the market. If they were handsome Clea did not care whether or not they could act. The South of France was full of pretty young men, but this was not one of them. This man carried the label: dangerous.

Where was Clea, anyway? She glanced around the room, past the little clumps of whispering beautiful people, in her way as indifferent to their elegant Paris fashions, their jewels, their air of glossy confidence, as the newcomer in the doorway.

'Where's your mama?' Sam Ransom loomed up beside her, swirling a glass in his hand so that ice-cubes tinkled like bells. 'She'll love the new arrival. This I want to see ...' There was malice in his voice. He had a grudge against Clea at the moment. One of the barbed questions he asked in his last interview had brought him a glass of Martini flung full into his face. Why the oddly expectant tone, though? Who was the newcomer? Sam knew him, that was obvious, which meant he was newsworthy, but then who at Clea's parties was not?

Except herself. The wry addition flashed into her mind and she smiled to herself.

'Clea's temper better today?' Sam sounded touchy. He would not get over Clea's fit of rage for a long time. Clea's temper was famous. Sweet as honey most of the time, she could flare up suddenly and turn into a tigress, the wonderful violet eyes flashing, the warm mouth as tight as a trap. It was one of the qualities which made her newsworthy, apart from her incredible beauty. Unpredictability gave her an electric charge other actresses lacked and it was unfair of Sam to protest at something which made Clea so eminently good copy to him and his kind.

'Ben, you got here! That's great!' A loud, burring voice cut through the ceaseless babble of voices in the crowded room, and Joanne watched as Lester Swann waddled towards the stranger in the door, his enormous hand held out in welcome. Lester was one of the money men behind Clea's new film. An American based in France for tax purposes, his fortune made in industry, spending his cushioned retirement in amusing himself and trying to make yet more money by gambling on the film industry, Lester was an old friend of Clea's.

So the dark-eyed stranger was a friend of Lester's, was he? That placed him at once in a separate bracket.

Although Lester moved in film circles now he reserved this warm appreciation for those of his own world. His manner to actors was just faintly condescending, as though they were children whom he humoured and found amusing.

She watched as the dark man allowed Lester to draw him into the party. The smile on his hard mouth was purely polite, never reaching his eyes, which remained sardonic and contemptuous as he shook hands with the people Lester ferried up to meet him. From the attitude of those around the little group, Joanne guessed that the newcomer was wealthy, influential, someone to be reckoned with in the film world. She was accustomed to sitting here, speculating quietly about those around her. It was her way of enjoying the party.

The french windows had been flung open to admit the soft night air. A faint summer breeze wafted the fragrance of the garden into the room, dispelling the stale odour of drink and cigarette smoke which the party had built up over the past hour. Joanne sat in a corner, partly shielded by floor-length white velvet curtains. Clea had a passion for surrounding herself with blue and white—her colours, she called them, knowing how they set off her beauty, deepening the blue of her eyes, emphasising the black hair which still revealed no trace of silver. Gossip whispered that her hairdresser saw to that, but Joanne knew that it was a lie. Clea needed no artificial aid to keep her hair black. Time had so far laid no unkindly hand on it.

'I think it would look quite distinguished, actually, darling,' she had said once, smiling impishly. 'I shall grow old very gracefully.'

Joanne had smiled back. 'Well, I see no signs of it so far.'

'Darling!' Clea had said on a husky note, patting her cheek, grateful for the reassurance, although surely her mirror told her as much whenever she looked into it.

Lester was talking loudly, his slightly protuberant blue eyes swivelling round the room. 'But where is she? Where's Clea? You must meet her, Ben, she's as fantastic as she looks on screen.' His eyes fell upon Joanne in her withdrawn corner and a slightly puzzled look crossed his face. It was quite common for people to stare at Joanne in that way. Although she was always to be seen in Clea's wake, few people remembered her, or her relationship to Clea. There was sufficient of a likeness between them for a second, curious glance, but Joanne was aware that the features which in Clea added up to startling beauty, in herself came to something far less eye-catching.

She was accustomed to it, so when Lester looked at her in that puzzled way, she was not surprised and replied to his smile with one of her own, unoffended. The man beside him had followed his glance. Joanne met the cold probe of his eyes, experiencing a stab of hostility. Who the hell did he think he was? She returned his sardonic stare with resentment. One of his thin brows flicked upward. He ran those cool eyes over her once, then dismissed her with an indifferent movement of his wide shoulders. The look, the movement, infuriated her.

She was hardened to being ignored by the satellites revolving around her mother, but for some reason the cold rejection of this total stranger pricked at her ego, bringing a flush to her face and a tension to her body.

Staring at him, she noted the expensive cut of his dark suit; the gloss of luxury he exuded, from his thick black hair to his polished black shoes. Conservative clothes, she thought. That indicated something about his personality. His blue-striped shirt was immaculate. Hardly suitable for a party, however. He looked as if he had just strolled out of a city board room; formal, expensive. He should have looked out of place among the dazzlingly clad guests. It was maddening that somehow he contrived to make it appear that everyone else was out of place, asserting his own stamp upon the occasion through sheer assurance.

Glancing around the room she was both amused and annoyed to see how many of the women were looking at him sideways, assessing and coveting him. Most of the businessmen she had ever met had been heavily built, conditioned by their sedentary occupation. This man was lithely built, his body as tough as his hard-boned face, his physical build suggesting athleticism and strength. Some people moved between herself and Lester's group and she lost sight of them for a moment until another movement gave her a view of that arrogant black head, turned in profile towards her, the features as sharp as new-minted coins. She looked away, angry to catch herself watching him so intently.

When she looked back the obscuring guests had moved off and she could see him clearly again. Out of the crowd swam Lina Rothman, her red hair glinting under the chandelier, her slanting eyes lazily smiling.

'Lester, honey,' she murmured, her hand touching his arm, while those green eyes looked at his companion. 'How are you?'

Lester admired her, was resigned to her open interest in the man with him. 'Lina, this is Ben Norris,' he said, half sad, half amused.

'Jeb Norris's son?' There was a peculiar brightness in Lina's surprised eyes, a curiosity in her stare as she held out a hand to him.

Joanne had picked up the name and was startled. Jeb Norris's son, she thought, staring at him. Good lord! And Lester had brought him to Clea's party? Was he mad? Or didn't he know? It was, of course, an old story, possibly forgotten by most people. There had been so much scandal to overlay it in the past twenty years. Clea had always been good material for the gossips and none of her romances had been hidden from the public gaze. She lived right out in the open as though under a footlight. But none of the later stories had been as fascinating as the duel Jeb Norris fought over her on the beach at Santa Anna. It had held the headlines for days. Jeb Norris had been hurt enough to spend a week in hospital. His opponent had escaped unscathed and victorious, had married Clea a month later in England.

Joanne stared at the dark head of Jeb Norris's son. From what she had seen of his father's face in newspapers, there was a distinct resemblance, but newsprint blurred features and gave a grey uniformity to faces.

She had been born a year after the duel. She had once had a first-hand account of it from her father, the victor. His voice had been wry with self-mockery as he gave her his version. She had listened, wide-eyed. Even at that age Clea had seemed to her like a fairy princess, and the duel had seemed just the sort of event which one might expect in the life of so marvellous a creature as her mother. Her father, John Ross, had wearied of the travelling circus which was life with Clea. He stuck it for five years and towards the end, Joanne suspected, it had been largely for her sake that he had stayed.

By then, Clea had fallen out of love with him and he with her. The divorce had come as no surprise to anyone, even Joanne. Her father had gently explained it to her, laying no shadow of blame upon Clea, and she was grateful to him for that later. He had asked if she would prefer to live with her mother or himself, and Joanne had cried, because the choice was too painful for her to make. She had felt bitterly that they neither of them had the right to ask her to make it. Clea had come into her nursery, perfumed and silken, all softness and warmth, and taken her into her arms, stroking her hair. 'My baby stays with me,' she had said decidedly, and John Ross had not argued.

There had been no violent upheavals for Joanne to weather. Everyone was calmly civilised and when her father had vanished from their lives things went on much as they had before.

John Ross had flown back to England and married again; a calm, pleasant, polite Englishwoman, as different from Clea as chalk from cheese. The marriage had been a very happy one. They had produced two children, David and Patricia, nice, polite, fair children whom Joanne had met whenever she visited her father.

She had found nothing in common with them, nor they with her. Their world was so far removed from her own that they were like creatures from another planet.

Towards her father Joanne felt quiet affection. The one madness of his whole life had been his brief infatuation with Clea. Over that, he had behaved uncharacteristically, spurred into a wild romanticism. After the divorce he returned to his true character, sinking himself in his family business. He ran the large London hotel his father had left him with calm efficiency. He was well-to-do, efficient, kind. Joanne often wished she cared more for him, but all her affection had long ago been poured at her mother's feet.

Glancing back at Lester's circle, she found that Lina Rothman had captured Ben Norris's attention, exerting all her powers of fascination, which were considerable, the green eyes lifted to his face, a beckoning smile on her mouth. Lina was five years younger than Clea and far less famous. She could act, however, Joanne admitted wryly. Clea had never been able to act. She had never needed to—her beauty had dominated every scene she played, extinguishing all other women.

Ben Norris was looking back at Lina with an unreadable expression. When he spoke his voice was too low for Joanne to pick up his words, but she could read the irony in his eyes very clearly as Lina signalled an unspoken invitation to him.

What was he doing here tonight? Curiosity? Had he come to see the woman over whom his father had lost his head years ago?

He was around thirty, she estimated. He must have been a little boy of seven or eight when the duel took place. Old enough to have known of it, no doubt. She knew from her own experience how much children pick up of what is going on around them in the adult world which people assume wrongly is above their heads.

His mother, Linda Norris, had been an actress, too, she seemed to remember, although she had never become famous. Joanne recalled gossip about her vaguely. Drinking, wild behaviour, fits of violence—how much of it had been her husband's fault and how much her own was not clear. What was clear was that Ben Norris must have had a pretty rotten childhood, with a wild mother and a father who had committed social suicide by making a fool of himself in public over a notorious film star.

By now she sensed that all the guests were aware of his identity. Eyes watched him remorselessly. He appeared unaware of, or indifferent to, their curiosity. A glass in his hand, he lounged carelessly, listening to Lina without a flicker of self-awareness. She was talking smilingly, one red-taloned hand flexing on his arm as though she were feeling his muscles—and, Joanne grimaced, there was no doubt about the existence of muscles beneath that smooth-tailored sleeve.

Suddenly Clea materialised in the french windows. She had been wandering around the brightly lit gardens with a small troupe of male admirers, Joanne guessed. Now she posed, framed in the white velvet curtains, her beauty staggering, the warm curves of her body daringly exposed in the white gown she wore.

Only a woman of supreme self-confidence would have chosen to wear a gown of such classical simplicity.

Only a great beauty could have got away with it at her age. Joanne felt, as she always did, a gasp of sheer wonder at her mother's loveliness. The violet eyes were framed in thick, black lashes, the depth and spacing of them superb. The pure oval of her face was framed in that sleek black hair, her lifted chin giving her throat a swan-like elegance. How, Joanne asked herself, did such very human material add up to such beauty? What did Clea have? Two eyes, a nose, a mouth, like every other woman. Yet on her it combined into one unit of extraordinary effect.

She wore around her neck a choker of black lace which cast a seductive shadow upon her white skin. Around one wrist glittered a thick bracelet of diamonds which flashed back the light from the chandeliers in a frozen rainbow of radiance. Clea never overloaded herself with jewellery, although her jewellery cases were crammed with precious stones. She had an unerring eye for the exact piece to wear. She might not be able to act, but nobody could fault her on her judgement on anything to do with the presentation of herself.

Quickly Joanne turned her head to glance at Ben Norris, and her eyes widened as she took in the expression on his face. She felt a stab of irritation. Didn't he know how he was staring? It was almost indecent, the expression on that handsome face. Everyone in the room was watching him.

Having made her usual entrance, well pleased with the effect of it, Clea moved forward. Lester Swann met her, beaming. Joanne heard his murmured words, saw her mother lift her head and look past him at the man in his wake. Clea bit her lip, obviously taken aback, and

Joanne could read the thoughts passing through her mind. Ben Norris, like herself, was a visible evidence of the passage of time, and although Clea pretended to be unafraid of the years she was as deeply, desperately afraid of age as any child of the dark.

Joanne felt a flash of pride in her courage as Clea held out her hand with a graceful, smiling gesture which covered the shock she had just received. Who said Clea could not act?

Ben Norris moved slowly forward to take it, his eyes riveted on Clea's face. The sardonic contempt had vanished. The coldness had gone. A look of incredulous admiration had taken their place. Ben Norris had come to sneer, to condemn. With one look, Clea had knocked him off balance.

He is human, after all, Joanne thought wryly. She watched with the rest of the room while Ben Norris took her mother's hand, staring down at her.

There was a pause. Total silence reigned. Then, apparently unaware of his audience, he slowly bent his black head in a movement of homage and kissed Clea's white hand.

Clea smiled.

Joanne saw the relief in her eyes, the relief one might feel when one was granted a reprieve from death. Ben Norris had capitulated without a struggle on first sight. Clea felt the triumph of it. She had not yet lost her ability to conquer a man without a word.

A faint sigh breathed round the room. Then people resumed their private conversations and the tide of talk swelled again.

The rest of the evening passed much as their parties

always did—in a babble of voices, laughter and music. Joanne came out of her corner from time to time to check on the quantity of food and drink. For several years now she had taken over the organisation of the household, first as deputy to her mother's secretary, Milly, and then as she grew more capable, taking over entirely.

A gorgon of fifty with sandy hair and fierce brown eyes, Milly's brusque manner masked a gentle spirit. Clea received an enormous post each day; fan mail, largely, but also a good deal of business letters. Milly had helped whenever it got out of proportion. Temporary girls came and went; Milly went on for ever, sharp of tongue, matter-of-fact, cool-headed. Only Clea and Joanne were aware that her prosaic exterior hid a vein of romanticism which had made her apply for a job with Clea in the first place. Her fondness for Clea was a secret between them all, one which Milly would hate to have exposed. Herself very plain, Milly worshipped the beauty of her employer without envy or malice, as one might that of a work of art. Clea was conscious of it, had come to rely on it. Milly's unfaltering affection was precious to her, and she returned the fondness freely.

Apart from Clea, the one person Milly cared about was Joanne herself. During her childhood, Milly had been the stable element in Joanne's life, a surrogate mother. Clea was often away filming in odd parts of the world. Milly had made sure Joanne had the home life a child needed, and Joanne responded by loving her deeply. She had seen strangers eyeing Milly with amusement as she moved around the villa in Clea's wake. They saw a stiff, sharp spinster in old-fashioned brown tweeds, blouses or twin sets, with a face bare of cosmetics and greying hair. They did not see how the whole household moved around her, or know how Clea depended upon her. It angered Joanne to see people dismiss Milly. They were so blinded by appearances that they could not see that beneath her gruffness lay a kindness, love and warmth which made her beautiful. That Clea should see it was another reason for loving Clea—at least she valued Milly at her real importance.

The guests began to leave. The volume of sound died down. Milly emerged from hiding and smiled at Joanne. 'Go well? How did the drink hold up?'

'It held,' Joanne said wrly. 'Just.'

Milly glanced over her shoulder and lifted a curious grey eyebrow towards where Ben Norris hovered beside Clea. 'New, isn't he? An actor? Who is he?'

'Jeb Norris's son.'

She watched Milly do a double-take, her brown eyes growing wide. 'Who on earth brought him here?'

'Lester Swann.'

'I might have guessed!' Milly was rueful.

'Either he doesn't know, or he's as thick as a plank!'

'Both,' said Milly; and they laughed. 'How did Clea take it when he appeared?'

'Shock for a moment,' Joanne said slowly, remembering the brief incident sharply. She laughed. 'She stood there like some blind goddess and he fell on his face.' Her tone held a strange astringency which she noted herself and could not account for, and Milly looked at her in surprised speculation.

'It gets harder for her each year,' said Milly, her face

holding a sweetness few had ever seen. 'Poor darling!'

'How old is she?' Joanne asked as she had many times before.

And as Milly had said many times before so now she said, 'As old as her hair and a little older than her teeth.'

'I sometimes feel older than her myself,' Joanne said without resentment.

'You're as young as you feel,' Milly told her in her wry, amused voice, her eyes smiling as she watched Joanne.

'I should get a telegram from the Queen congratulating me on my century, then,' Joanne yawned. 'It's four in the morning! I shall be dead tomorrow.' She glanced across at her mother. 'How does she do it? She looks exactly the way she did when the party started, not a hair out of place and her skin is dewy. Tomorrow while I'm crawling around with an ice-pack on my head, she'll be as fresh as a daisy.'

'Years of getting up at first light to go to the studio, even after a party the night before,' Milly grunted. 'Clea has learnt how to grab a catnap at any hour of the day or night.'

Everyone had gone now. Only Ben Norris remained, leaning on the wall, his head propped on his hand, his dark eyes intent on Clea's laughing face.

'He looks as if he doesn't know what's hit him,' Milly muttered. 'Shall I break it up or will you? Clea should get some sleep.'

'I will,' said Joanne, walking over to them. Clea turned her black head to smile at her, putting an arm affectionately around her shoulders. 'Have you met my little girl, Ben?'

He seemed to Joanne to detach his eyes from her mother's face with slow reluctance. He turned his head and looked indifferently at Joanne. 'No,' he said, and she felt he might as well have added, 'And I don't want to now.'

'My daughter, Joanne,' Clea said, hugging her. 'Don't you think she's like me, Ben?'

The thin brows arched. He ran his dark eyes slowly, consideringly, dismissively over Joanne and she felt her cheeks begin to burn under his stare.

'No,' he said, and she was so angry she could have hit him. Many people introduced to her would stare incredulously, then pretend to find a likeness. She knew they were lying and it irritated her. But it smoothed the first encounter. Ben Norris had made no attempt to be polite. He stated bluntly what his cold eyes had already told her. He found her a pale, uninteresting shadow beside Clea. The colouring Clea had bestowed on her at birth was all she had to show for her relationship with her mother. Whatever chemistry created the magical allure of Clea Thorpe had not worked for her daughter. Joanne was hardly plain, but she was scarcely beautiful. Her withdrawn personality underlined her looks. People glanced at her and away, often without ever having registered her at all, and they often failed to remember her when they met her again.

A slender, brown-skinned girl with long, straight black hair falling to her shoulders and eyes which lacked the depth of colour which made Clea's so bewitching, in the shadow of her mother she was almost invisible.

To cover her anger, she asked Ben Norris, 'Are you staying in Nice?'

'For a few weeks.'

'At a hotel?' She could sense his impatient thoughts as she asked. He did not want to talk to her, to answer polite questions. His voice was curt as he replied, as if he wished her miles away.

'A villa.'

Clea picked up the words. 'Whose, darling?' She knew everyone worth knowing in the district. She had owned the Villa Jessamine for ten years, spending her free time here whenever she could, and her parties were famous, invitations to them much sought after.

'Lester's,' he said, turning back to her, his eyes on the delicate contours of her face. Even now there was something of the little girl about Clea, which, combined with the tender sweetness of her eyes and mouth, made her memorable even without the addition of that extra dimension which adds up to beauty. Providence, when giving out its gifts at birth, had opened a positive cornucopia for Clea Thorpe. She had never known what it was to lack anything; love, money, success had showered down on her from early childhood.

'Lester's my angel,' she said, laughing. 'He's going to back my next film.'

'He suggested I might like to invest in it,' Ben Norris told her, watching her.

'And shall you?' Clea asked the question lightly, without pressure, and all of them knew the answer even before she had finished asking it.

'It's an attractive idea,' he said, but the evasive reply

did not fool Clea. Her eyes shone at him, gentle, inviting. Clea was always honeyed to the money men.

'It is a good part,' she said, sighing.

There had been some delays over the film. Joanne did not know why. Clea had not worked for some months, but that was good. She needed a holiday.

Now at least she understood Lester's eager welcome to him. Ben would be a wealthy man. Jeb Norris had made millions in the States in the electronic field. It seemed to Joanne only just that some of that money should fertilise the film world. There had been so many men in her mother's life, and most of them with fortunes. They all seemed to run together into a common face, a common destiny. They had come and gone, shooting through their lives like comets through a night sky, leaving little to remind anyone of their existence, except that most of them had ploughed money into Clea's career. Some of them had made fortunes with her films; others had lost fortunes. Jeb Norris, Joanne suspected, had once invested in a film for Clea, and newspapers had hinted that his gamble with her career had been another cause for his wife's jealous tempers.

'When do you go back to school?' he asked her suddenly, and she flushed. He could hardly have been nastier if he had tried! She had never imagined herself to be a beauty, but she had not thought she looked like a schoolgirl.

Clea laughed in a silvery fashion which masked irritation. 'Oh, I need Joanne at home with me,' she said, not bothering to mention that 'her little girl' was twenty years old, soon to be twenty-one. Any mention of age was taboo in this household. The clock has stopped, Joanne thought. Time has frozen in a silver waterfall. Clea is ageless, unchanging.

I feel like the Lady of Shalott, she told herself. I have sat here for a long time looking at life through the mirror of Clea's eyes and I am very tired of my elegant captivity.

Ben Norris was staring at her. She saw that he was trying to estimate her age. It would not be easy for him. She wore little make-up, even at parties. Her sun-bronzed skin really looked better without it, and Clea did not like it. The straight blue dress, chosen for her by Clea, added to the illusion which her mother desired, freezing her at the age of sixteen or so, and her slender body and straight hair made that illusion more convincing.

Milly joined them, having given up hope that Joanne would ever achieve the objective.

Clea caught her look and smiled at her. 'This is Milly,' she informed Ben tenderly. 'My dragon, my guardian! She rules my life with a rod of iron, and I fancy she's come to send me to bed.'

The little-girl submission was charming. He smiled at her as if entranced. 'Must you?'

'I need my beauty sleep,' she pouted.

He shook his black head. 'Not you.'

'How nice,' said Clea, and watched him take her hand and kiss it. 'Why, anyone would think you had French blood! Your father was never so gallant.' She lingered, her lashes hiding her eyes. 'How is he, by the way?' The way in which he was mentioned made it clear that she had not spoken of him before.

'Fine,' Ben said, brusqueness in his voice.

'He's in the States, I suppose?'

Ben hesitated. 'I imagine so,' he said. 'We rarely see each other.'

Clea turned away, smiling. 'Well, goodnight, Ben.'

The pure white silk fluttered around her slim body as she walked away, every movement attracting the eye. Milly followed her, although Clea's maid, Marie, would be waiting in the bedroom, despite the late hour. Clea never put herself to bed. Like royalty, she expected to be waited on hand and foot, but she had the gift of inspiring loyalty and service in other women. Unlike other stars of her calibre, she had a warm, easy-going nature. Other women found it surprisingly easy to like her. She was never spiteful, never cruel, never mean. Her childlike fear of age made her pitiable. It was her only real vice, her only approach to cruelty. Even the men in her life still retained affection for her after she left them, and her departure was usually because, with a child's eye for novelty, she had been drawn to a new love while never quite deserting the old. Lovers became friends, and Clea nourished those friendships, keeping them alive with telephone calls, letters, Christmas cards.

Joanne turned to Ben Norris politely. 'I'll show you out,' she said.

He gave her a hostile glance. 'Thank you.' She wondered if his antagonism, which had been plain to her from that first cold look, was due to the fact that she was her father's daughter, a reminder of the humiliating duel his father had fought against hers.

'How long do you and your mother plan to stay in Nice?'

'Another fortnight at least.'

'And then where?'

She shrugged. 'The States, for a script conference on the new film, then on location in Spain, I think.'

'I'd like to watch some of the location work,' he said casually.

Her mouth twisted wryly. 'Would you?'

He gave her an icy look, interpreting her tone correctly. 'If I am to invest money in this film I shall want to know what I'm getting.'

She almost told him, but he looked as if he had no sense of humour, that hard, handsome face glacial. He would read her frankness for criticism of Clea—or worse, for jealousy. He would not understand that years of watching her mother play this game of love had made her cynical about it all. Clea needed to be surrounded with adoration. It was the breath of life to her. It fed the springs of her self-confidence, kept her young. Joanne had never known what it was to resent her mother's ability to make men tumble like ninepins. She had never been in love herself. She had never lost a man to Clea and she had no intention of ever doing so. To avoid that catastrophe she had surrounded herself with a hedge of thorns, like the Sleeping Beauty, and slept behind them determined never to awake.

There had never been any moment in which she made a conscious decision about it. From girlhood she had somehow drifted into the situation, and now she knew she would never compete with her beautiful mother for any man. The pain such a clash would inflict would ruin any romance. She strongly suspected that Clea, although she loved her, would be unable to resist a display of strength if she saw any man turning towards Joanne. She might love Clea, but she knew her through and through. Clea would blindly try to steal any man who showed interest in her daughter because she would see it as the beginning of the end for her.

Joanne had seen *Snow White* as a child and been taken out screaming hysterically by a concerned Milly after the wicked queen looked complacently at her own beauty in the mirror and asked 'Who is the fairest of them all?' The mirror's reply had torn the mask of beauty from the queen's face. Joanne had not known why she began to scream and sob, but years later the memory had flashed back and she had been struck by the incident. Perhaps even as a small child she had known that Clea's radiant loveliness might be terribly altered towards her if ever she competed with her.

They walked outside into the sunrise. The sky was a gentle opal shot with gold and rose, the fluffy white clouds lined with diffused brightness. Far below them lay the coastal strip, the palm trees dark oars moving in a faint breeze. She inhaled pleasurably, her fatigue forgotten in the beauty of the morning.

Ben Norris stood beside her, staring over the gardens with their manicured green lawns, faintly pearled with dew, their carefully trimmed hedges and trees, their regimented flowers. 'A chocolate box cover,' he said ironically.

She tensed with irritation. 'It's beautiful,' she said. She had always loved this view of Nice, the colourful roofs tumbling down to the blue sea, the geraniums in green pots, the white shutters and winding dusty roads, all held in a quality of light which made it a painter's dream.

Turning, she was struck suddenly by the hard lines of his face, the cheekbones austere beneath their covering of brown skin. He did not look the sort of man who tumbled off his pedestal the moment he set eyes on a woman, yet he had done so tonight, as public a confession of infatuation as his father's duel over Clea twenty-two years ago, and when he remembered that and did some sums, wouldn't he feel a fool, losing his head over a woman old enough to have captivated his father so long ago?

She had the feeling that Ben Norris was not a man who would enjoy looking a fool. There was arrogance in the lift of that black head, the twist of his mouth.

He turned, as if sensing her gaze, and looked at her. His eyes were almost black, resisting the probe of the sun, their heavy lids half hooding them. 'How often does she have these parties?' he asked her, and there was a strange echo of sardonic comment in his voice.

'Occasionally,' she said, then, defensively, 'After all, she isn't working at the moment.'

'No,' he said softly, 'she isn't, is she?' The dark eyes skimmed her body again in silent insolence and her hands tightened at her side.

'You're a changeling,' he said suddenly, his mouth mocking. 'I can scarcely believe you're her daughter.'

Joanne felt her skin burn. 'I take after my father,' she said curtly.

She saw a flash light the dark eyes as if mention of

her mother's husband could annoy him. 'They were divorced years ago, weren't they?'

'Yes,' she said, her temper at boiling point. 'I think Clea was cured of marrying them after my father. Marriage only adds to the problems when you split.'

'Adds to the alimony, too,' he said unpleasantly. 'Only I suppose she earns too much for that to matter.' His eyes pinned her down as if she were a moth on a card. 'Are you jealous of her?'

She glared at him. 'No, I am not! I wouldn't want any of the specimens she picks up.' Her blue eyes flashed with rage, giving them a brightness they rarely had, and his eyes narrowed on her, reading her message clearly.

'Is that a dart aimed for me?' She did not answer and he laughed harshly. 'It missed its target, sweetheart.' He climbed into a low-slung sports car parked nearby and shot away with a roar which deafened her.

Joanne felt sick. What on earth had possessed her to give way to a fit of temper? She didn't care whether or not Ben Norris had fallen for Clea. She had seen it all before. She was used to it. Why had she let fly like that?

Milly wandered out and smiled at her questioningly. 'Something wrong?'

'I've a headache,' she lied, although come to think of it, it was not a lie, because her head was definitely aching now.

'Some air will cure that,' Milly said, adding drily, 'Sleep wouldn't hurt, either.'

'I'll go to bed in a moment.'

Milly looked down over Nice with a sigh. 'That view

... it gets better every time I see it.' She held a hand over her mouth, yawning. 'Strange, Jeb Norris's boy turning up. He seemed smitten with her, didn't he?'

'It must be in his blood,' said Joanne, pleased with herself for sounding so cool.

'Jeb was her first love,' Milly said, sounding nostalgic. 'She lit up like a Christmas tree when he walked into a room. I always liked him. He was quite a man.' She gave Joanne a fond smile. 'Your father was a nice man, but no Jeb Norris.'

'Why did Clea marry my father and not Jeb Norris?'

Milly sighed. 'His wife used that boy as a weapon against her. Jeb loved the boy, couldn't bear the idea of losing him, and his wife would have taken the boy away if he left her.'

'How did the duel fit in?'

Milly laughed. 'Oh, that! Clea loved the idea. Jeb was jealous because your father was paying her too much attention. They called it a fencing match to stop police interference, but everyone knew there was more to it than that. Jeb thought he'd win ... he was sure of it, and if he did, your father would have gone away, but Jeb slipped on a piece of seaweed and broke his leg.'

'Very romantic,' Joanne muttered, angry again. What a pair of fools the two men must have been!

'While Jeb was in hospital your father ran off with Clea.' Milly smiled. 'The boy looks like his father. A very handsome man, Jeb Norris, charming, too, with a smile that could coax birds off trees.'

'His son hasn't inherited *that*,' Joanne said sharply.

Milly laughed. 'Oh, I don't know ... he's worth

more than a second glance. Clea seemed very taken with him.'

'He's fifteen years younger than her!' Joanne muttered, head bent, mouth twisted.

Milly looked at her oddly. 'Don't be angry with her ... she can't help it, any more than the cat can help stealing birds.'

Joanne snorted with half-manic laughter, imagining Clea as a silken cat stalking off with Ben Norris. Her face tightened again. Clea would soon strip away his feathers. By now most of Nice would know that Jeb Norris's son had fallen like a ton of bricks for Clea Thorpe, and the tongues would be wagging violently. He must learn to accept the notoriety which a love affair with Clea brought upon its victim. Why should she care? Other men had gone that way before him, and it would even, she told herself bitterly, be amusing to watch that proud dark head brought low as the gossip flowed over him. It would serve him right.

CHAPTER TWO

At sunrise the beach below the villa was always empty. The flat golden sands were printless and virginal, the calm blue water flowing up on to them in a gentle wave which was almost silent. The only sound was the melancholy cry of the gulls.

Joanne usually walked there each morning. She loved the silence and beauty of the sea at dawn, the limitless horizon offering a freedom which her nature sought hopelessly. It was such a contrast to the chaotic, brittle life Clea seemed to prefer. Often she got there before the sun arose and saw it come up from the horizon in a drifting mist of opalescent colour, fire-shot with orange, blue and gold, and stood watching it with dreaming eyes.

This morning she had walked as usual down from the villa along the private cliff path, between shady trees which made a dark gorge for her to follow, their branches moving softly overhead in the morning breeze. The rocky path was slippery with dark green moss, spongy underfoot. The sides glistened with water which trickled down from some subterranean spring buried deep in the cliffs.

At her heels scampered Harry, a rough-haired Jack Russell terrier, his short legs deft as he made his way over the rock, his eyes bright between his white hair. Harry had once caught a rabbit on the path and had hoped for years to repeat this feat. Hope sprang eternal in his canine breast.

Emerging on the beach, Joanne halted in surprise and consternation to find herself for once not the only human being in sight.

Ben Norris walked there, his black head bent, his hands driven into his pockets. She would have retreated the way she had come, but Harry, seeing one of the master race in view, raced forward, barking at him delightedly.

Ben stopped, looked round, and grinned as he caught sight of Harry's cheerful face. The little dog's ecstatic welcome was infectious. Ben bent, rubbing the wiry head, and Harry licked his hands, squirming with joy.

Watching the movements of that long-fingered hand as it fondled the dog's ears, Joanne felt a sharp pang. She thought of those hands touching herself and shivered, then caught herself up with irritated contempt. Why on earth had she thought like that? There was not even the slightest excuse and she was furious with herself.

Ben had not noticed her. She was standing in the shadows at the end of the cliff path, out of sight, but now she moved forward and he looked round.

'He wants you to throw a stick for him,' she said as casually as if they often met there.

Ben shot her a frowning look. 'Oh, hello. Is he your dog?'

'Yes,' she said, trying to sound bright and easy. 'His name is Harry.'

Her father had given him to her when she was fourteen and Clea had been furious because she thought animals were a nuisance and made a mess. Joanne had never had a pet before and she had been frantic to keep the tiny ball of white fluff which had been Harry aged two months.

Milly had said kindly, 'I'll make sure he keeps out of your way, Clea. He'll be no trouble.' And Clea had groaned but accepted his presence after that, going from one extreme to the other in time, so that now she doted on the bright-eyed little dog, although she got cross when he left his white hairs on her furniture and carpets, but he more than made up for that because some publicity shots of her cuddling him had been very popular. Clea looked sweet with Harry on her lap.

Ben looked down at the dog now, found a piece of

driftwood, while Harry capered about eagerly, and flung it into the sea. Barking excitedly, Harry flew after it, plunging into the sea, splashing violently as he swam towards the wood as it bobbed up and down on the crest of a wave.

Joanne glanced sideways at Ben. He had been a frequent visitor to the villa during the past week, but she had seen little of him. She knew better than to inflict her unwanted presence when Clea was entertaining a male guest. It was a lesson she had learnt at an early age. Clea would sometimes send for her to pose docilely on her lap while a strange man patted her cheek, said how like Clea she was, gave her a doll or some chocolates, and then she would be sent away with Milly before she became troublesome.

'You're up early,' she said.

'So are you.'

'I always am,' she shrugged. 'This is Harry's favourite time of day, his favourite walk. He lives to chase the seagulls.'

'Does he ever catch one?'

'No, thank goodness,' she said, watching the faint smile touch that hard mouth. 'They would eat him alive if he did. Have you ever really looked at those beaks?'

He glanced upward as a gull swooped overhead, the round eye brightly malevolent, the yellow beak cruelly curved. 'I wouldn't like to take one of them on,' he agreed. He pushed his hands back into his pockets. 'Your mother is still asleep, I suppose?'

'Clea gets up at ten.'

He shot her a frowning glance. 'Did you ever call her Mother?'

'No. She preferred me to use her name.' Clea dealt in images. She understood them. She did not want anyone having an image of her which was in any way maternal. It was, in her eyes, an ageing factor. It pinned on her a label she did not want.

Harry had retrieved the wood and waded out of the sea with it in his mouth. Dropping it at Ben's feet, he shook himself vigorously, showering Ben with salt drops.

'Hey, watch it,' she scolded. 'Sorry!' Ben ruefully brushed down his casual clothes. He was wearing cream pants and a dark brown shirt and Harry had left a trail of dark stains on both.

Bending, she picked up the stick and flung it with all her strength down the beach. Harry followed, yelping. 'That should take him a while,' she said, watching his short legs twinkling. 'Crazy idiot!'

Over the dog's running figure the seagulls circled, crying, making black shadows on the yellow sand, and the picture was memorable. She smiled, watching it, running her fingers through her long hair, unaware that the movement lifted her small breasts beneath the thin white cotton shirt, giving her a sudden grace. The man looked sharply at her, his eyes running down over the slender body.

'How old are you?' he asked abruptly.

She looked round at him in surprised, blank reaction. 'Twenty,' she said. 'Twenty-one next month.'

His skin reddened and she knew she had taken him

aback, had shocked him. He had believed her to be almost a child. He was around six foot, towering over her, and she felt smaller than ever beside him. There was incredulity and anger in the dark eyes as he stared at her, as though she had affronted him by claiming an age she did not possess.

'Ask Milly,' she said, almost mockingly. Why should she lie about her age? He only had to check up. Her birth had been something of an event in the gossip columns.

He knew she was making fun of him. His eyes narrowed and something in his look alarmed her. She turned and ran away, the wind lifting her dark hair, winnowing it, like cool fingers. She felt a peculiar apprehension, as though he might follow her, as though she was running from him in half fear, half excitement. But he made no effort to follow, standing there, staring after her.

She and Harry made their way back to the villa up the cliff path. It was a stiff climb and she was breathless by the time they were emerging in the garden. She had climbed as though the devil were after her and her heart was racing. Flushed, dishevelled, she went into the house and found the housekeeper, Madame Lefeuvre, preparing Clea's breakfast. The tray lay on the table; a slim glass vase containing a single white rose, a silver pot of coffee, a jug of cream, some fruit and wafer-thin golden toast wrapped in a damask napkin. Clea always ate lightly.

'I'll take it up,' Joanne offered, and was given a quick smile.

'*Merci*, Joanne,' Madame said warmly. She had

known Joanne for years and was attached to her, a brusque Gallic woman despising easy expressions of affection, but her dark eyes full of warmth when she smiled.

It was an entirely female household. The women who worked for Clea were highly paid and had no tantrums to put up with, no insults to bear. Clea was a very good employer and she kept her staff year after year.

When Joanne entered the bedroom it was shadowy, filled with the fragrance of Clea's personal perfume. She crossed the deep-piled carpet and set down the tray, went over to open the blinds, so that the morning spilled into the room with sudden beauty.

Clea slept with a black velvet mask over her eyes. She stretched, yawning, the delicate white lace of her nightgown revealing perfect skin. How did she keep such textural magnificence at her age? Joanne wondered. Her throat showed no signs of wrinkling, her face was smooth as silk. Joanne bent to kiss her and Clea smiled, still masked.

'Darling! What time is it?'

'Just ten,' Joanne told her. 'A beautiful morning.'

Clea pulled off her mask and sat up. The huge violet eyes were bright in the flushed face. 'Have you been walking on the beach?'

'Yes,' Joanne said, thought of telling Clea she had seen Ben Norris there, then decided to stay silent about that.

Leaving her mother to enjoy a leisurely breakfast she changed into a bikini and went down to the pool to swim for an hour.

Floating on her back, she asked herself with irritation why she had not wanted to talk to Clea about Ben, but got no answer. She dived and swam, her movements concise and graceful, the black hair pinned on top of her head, enjoying the sun and the water.

She was still in the pool when she heard a step on the tiled surround and glanced up, shielding her eyes from the dazzle of the sun. A lean dark shadow was outlined against the sky.

'Energetic, aren't you?'

She felt her heart turn over and made no reply, swimming to the steps and hauling herself out of the water, shaking her black hair with the same sort of motion as Harry did when emerging from water.

Before she had time to dash into the changing room, Ben was beside her. She looked at him with antagonism and felt colour running into her face at the expression on his face.

The coral pink bikini altered her whole appearance. The slender, curved brown body was quite obviously that of a full-grown woman, not a child; the pleated cups leaving little of her small, high breasts to the imagination, the flat golden midriff and slim hips seductive against the elegantly proportioned legs.

'Well, well, well,' he murmured, lifting one of those dark brows.

Joanne blushed angrily. 'Excuse me while I get dressed.'

'Why bother?' he asked drily. 'You look very good just the way you are.'

She sidestepped to avoid him and he moved at the same moment so that she bumped into him, putting her wet palms against his chest to keep her balance in an instinctive movement.

His hands came up to her waist, holding her wet skin lightly. From a distance, she thought irrelevantly, it could look as though she were in his arms, and the idea sent her heartbeat spinning off into delirium. She had an incredulous suspicion that he had moved into her path quite deliberately.

Flickering an upward glance at him through her lashes, she said nervously, 'Please!'

'Please what?' he asked mockingly, and the dark eyes dropped to inspect her parted, surprised mouth. She hoped he could not hear the acceleration of her breathing. She had watched Clea flirting so often without ever playing that game herself and now she had no idea how to act, although she had a strong notion that Ben was flirting with her.

She pushed against his chest, trembling. He shrugged, as though suddenly bored with the game, stepped back and she fled, deeply aware of his eyes following her.

In the changing room she stared at her own reflection with numb amazement, seeing her skin burning with colour, her eyes hectic and a darker blue than she had ever seen before. Slowly she studied herself as if she had never seen her own body before, then turned away, her hands clenched at her side, as though she could not face whatever lay buried in her own eyes.

She dressed slowly and when she came out into the sunlight again there was no sign of him. The blue pool glimmered emptily in the morning light. Joanne walked to the house, her bare brown legs silky with half-dry dampness, her feet thrust into straw sandals, her slender body sheathed in very brief white shorts and a sleeveless T-shirt, her damp black hair hanging down her back.

He was with Clea in the white-and-gold drawing-room. Sleekly elegant in a white dress cut on the classical lines which suited her, Clea smiled at her as she entered. 'Ben's taking me to lunch in Nice, darling. Can you amuse yourself?'

'Of course,' Joanne said drily, avoiding his narrowed glance. He was lounging back in a chair, his lean body at ease, his hands behind his black head and although she barely looked his way she was deeply aware of the slow, methodical inspection of those cold eyes.

Clea's violet eyes skimmed over her too, and a faint line pleated her temples. 'Been swimming, darling?'

'Yes,' said Joanne, and Ben moved, swinging to his feet. She made a sudden, instinctive movement away from him without thinking, and his eyes shot to her face. Clea had turned towards the door and missed the brief incident. Ben paused, staring at Joanne, who looked at him with open antagonism, her black head lifted defiantly.

Milly came into the room just as they left it, and Joanne said to her flatly, 'They're lunching in Nice.'

'Mmm,' said Milly, mouth wry.

'Clea frowned at me,' Joanne told her. 'Do I look a mess?'

Milly sighed, staring at her. 'My dear girl, you look what you are ... a girl of twenty! Clea envies you.'

Joanne was incredulous. 'Clea? I don't believe it! How could she envy me anything?'

Milly's eyes were sad and loving. 'At your age you can afford to dash around without make-up, wearing the minimum of clothes—of course she envies you! She has to fight time every inch of the way. Don't you think she would love to relax as you do and enjoy life without remembering that she's always on public display?'

Joanne had never considered competing with her mother. The idea was ridiculous, painful. Milly watched her struggling with the thought and smiled affectionately.

'Come and help me with the fan mail,' she said. 'You can sort out the signed photographs while I do the letters.'

Joanne had always enjoyed that. Today, for some reason, she found herself looking at the glossy pictures of her mother with new eyes, seeing them in a novel light; the pale graining of the flawless skin, the shape of the features, the posed sweetness of the smile. Was it possible, she asked herself, that Ben was falling in love with Clea? The idea made her angry, which worried her, because she had never cared before when any man swung towards her mother like a magnetic needle pointing north, and why in God's name should she care about Ben Norris? He was a cold, arrogant stranger to her and the terrifying acceleration of her heartbeat when his hands rested on her body earlier was inexplicable. She rejected it. He had been flirting with her, playing a game, and only her own inexperience had made of the brief moment anything worth remembering.

Lester Swann was giving a party that evening, a

rather smaller, more intimate affair than that which Clea had given. Joanne went into Nice that afternoon and bought herself a new dress in a wild flicker of rebellion which she herself found puzzling.

She had meant to buy something slightly more adult, but when she found herself in a smart little boutique in one of the narrow alleys in the town, she was caught by a dress which was totally unsuitable and even as she tried on others of more discreet colouring, her eyes again and again returned to the flame-coloured dress displayed on a small stand in the shop. The assistant, smiling, said, 'Go on, try it!'

Joanne laughed, shaking her head, but let herself be persuaded, and when she saw herself in the dress she knew she had to have it. The girl sighed over it. 'Oh, you look fabulous!' She was a small, dark French girl with olive skin and Joanne guessed she loved the dress herself. It would be way above her pocket. The price shocked Joanne, but by then she would not have cared if it had cost twice as much.

For the first time, Joanne wore noticeable make-up. When she came downstairs Milly turned and did a visible double-take. Joanne flushed, holding her head high.

'Well, I am nearly twenty-one, after all,' she said with self-conscious anxiety.

'Did I say a word?'

'You didn't have to ... your face said it all.'

'It isn't my face you have to worry about!'

'Why should she object? Who's going to notice me?'

Milly's mouth twisted ironically. 'In that dress?

You're kidding!' She looked over the bright flame of the tight-bodiced, full-skirted dress with lifted eyebrows. It had a Spanish look, the skirts cascading in tiers to her feet, the waist tiny, the bodice outlining her high breasts. She gave Joanne a sharp, curious look. 'Who do you want to notice you?'

Joanne felt her face burn, 'Nobody!'

'Then that,' said Milly, 'is the wrong dress to wear, because as sure as God made little apples, men are going to notice you tonight.'

Clea came into the room accompanied by the sweet fragrance which always floated around her, the perfume she always wore, a French one created for her years ago.

Joanne turned slowly, bracing herself for the comments she expected. She had made her first gesture of rebellion, and she felt as uncertain as a baby taking its first steps.

Clea's eyes widened and for a long moment they stared at each other across the room. Milly folded her hands, watching, her manner unreadable.

Clea's face had a mask-like formality. Joanne had a terrifying urge to run from the room, tear off the dress and return herself to the old, schoolgirlish way of dressing. She had made the gesture on impulse and now she was regretting it, afraid of what she might have unleashed.

Milly moved to Clea and made a big thing of adjusting a fold of her dress, her eyes on Clea's face. 'Our girl is growing up,' she said in her gruff voice. 'Of course, she'll never be another Clea Thorpe, but we love her just the way she is, don't we?'

Clea's face altered. The terrible stillness went out of it. Her lips trembled. 'Yes,' she said unsteadily, taking a deep breath. 'Darling, you do look very grown up.'

Joanne's shoulders relaxed from the tension which had held them. She searched her mother's eyes and Clea smiled sweetly, her lashes falling to hide the expression in them.

Clea had a sleek white Rolls, luxurious and ultra-comfortable. She liked to drive it herself at times, although she had a chauffeur, Donald, who lived with his wife above the garage and spent most of his time in polishing the three cars Clea owned.

Today Clea drove and they shot down the narrow, winding road between dusty hillsides thick with cypress and olive trees. Below, Joanne could see through the branches the blue waters of the sea, glittering in the sunlight, and the beach was still alive with people. Some young men flung a large yellow ball between them, their sunburned bodies lithe as they ran to and fro. The sun was setting slowly, still warm on their skin. As the car descended, the sun sank, making a crimson path across the water, like a lighthouse beam. People were leaving the beach in throngs now, but the young men went on playing, their shadows black on the yellow sand.

Clea was wearing a black dress tonight, her throat wound round with diamonds in a gold setting. A white fur wrap was flung around her shoulders. Above it, her hair shone like black silk, framing the delicate oval of her face. She was silent as she drove, but once or twice she shot Joanne an unreadable look, as though she were inwardly speculating on her behaviour.

When they arrived at Lester's villa, Joanne followed her into the house. Lester met them, bending reverently over Clea's hand, but for once he gave Joanne a startled, seeing look and smiled at her with appreciation. She followed them into the party. Ben came forward, cutting a swathe through the other men effortlessly, and took Clea away. Joanne knew he had not even seen her, and the sinking depression that thought caused made her angry with herself. She stood watching, her fingers curled into her palms, and wished to God she had not bought the flame dress or worn it tonight.

'Do my eyes deceive me? Can it really be the little girl who never grew up?' asked a familiar voice behind her, and she turned with a start to look at Sam Ransom's incredulous face.

'Oh, hello, Sam,' she said flatly. He lived in Nice, writing a daily column for one of the popular London newspapers, filling it with titbits of gossip which he picked up at parties like these. A man in his early thirties, Sam was quick-witted, charming, opportunistic, and she knew that any unguarded remark she let slip could make the newspapers next day. She was always careful what she said to Sam.

He was looking her over with amused interest. 'What's this? A touch of rebellion at last? How did the great star take it?'

She felt herself blushing and pretended to laugh. 'How's your wife?' she asked deliberately.

'Ouch,' he said, grimacing. He had been divorced by his wife a year earlier and she knew that the subject was one he still avoided. Sam had, she suspected, cared for his wife more than he would ever admit. His brown eyes glinted. 'When did you grow claws, sweetheart? And I always thought you were such a sweet little girl.'

'So I am,' she said. 'To my friends.'

'And I'm not one of them?' He quirked a lazy eyebrow upward.

'Prove it,' she said.

He laughed. 'You won't use your claws on me if I don't use mine on you, is that it?'

'That seems fair enough,' she shrugged.

He grinned suddenly, his eyes altering. 'Okay, princess. Can I get you a drink?'

'Thank you,' she said, smiling back. Sam was one of the few people who ever seemed aware of her. They had had a long relationship of friendly neutrality and she felt at ease with him.

He slipped away and returned in a moment with a glass of champagne. She sipped it, her eyes on her glass, and Sam looked down at her in a considering way.

'Your figure is developing along interesting lines,' he said, his head to one side. 'When did this happen? Or is it just that very sexy dress you're wearing?'

'It might be your eyesight,' she snapped, and Sam laughed, his eyes sparkling.

'Oh, no, sweetie, my eyesight is fine.' He leered at her teasingly. 'Shall we dance? I can't wait to find out if you feel as good as you look.' He took the glass from her hand, put it down and whisked her off to dance before she had a chance to protest.

There was a crush of other people in the room and they were unavoidably pushed close, Joanne's black head against his shoulder. He tightened his grip on her waist and she looked up in protest.

She found the lazy interest of his eyes embarrassing and knew he could see her uneasiness. His smile deepened. 'You know, you're a very strange girl,' he said. 'I had you down in my book as a little puritan, but puritans don't have mouths like yours.'

She was about to slap him down when over his shoulder her eye caught Ben's narrowed gaze and she felt her heart flip over sickeningly. She forced her face to disguise the reaction she had felt, her eyes drifting over him without expression, then looked back at Sam. Lowering her lashes, she asked sweetly, 'Mouths like what?'

Sam watched her curiously. 'Come out into the garden and I'll show you.'

She lifted her lashes and looked at him. 'Is that a new version of let me show you my etchings?'

'That comes later,' he said, grinning, and she laughed back.

'I wouldn't trust you further than I could see you.'

'A sound principle,' he agreed. 'But you have to learn some time.'

'Maybe I'd choose another tutor.'

Sam bent his head rapidly and took a light kiss. He closed his eyes. 'Mmm . . . promising.'

'For you or for me?'

'Both of us,' he said, his eyes impudent.

Joanne was finding the game exhilarating. It was the first time in her life she had ever played it and she was finding it easy to keep the ball in the air, her eyes bright as she looked back at Sam's interested appreciative face.

'Is it true Jeb Norris is in Nice?' he asked abruptly, and her smile died on her mouth.

'What?' She was so shattered that she had no thought of concealing it from his needle-sharp eyes.

'You didn't know?' Sam stared at her. 'That's revealing.'

'What makes you think he is?' she asked tensely.

'A little bird told me.'

'He could have got it wrong.'

Sam shook his head. 'No, the source is impeccable. Apparently, Jeb Norris came over on a big yacht ... it tied up early this morning and he came ashore. I thought he'd be here tonight.'

She glanced involuntarily towards Ben and found him watching her, his dark face enigmatic. Clea was standing beside him talking to Lester, her laughter audible, a glass in her hand. Joanne looked at her mother anxiously.

'Someone ought to break the news to her,' Sam said thoughtfully, following her gaze. 'If Jeb Norris walks in without warning, Clea is going to get a shock.'

'No,' said Joanne, turning her head back to him, 'don't!' And, at his quick, surprised stare, she added huskily, 'Please, Sam.' She knew she could not bear the idea of Sam walking up to them and telling them Jeb had arrived. She did not want to see Ben's face, although she did not quite know what she expected him to do or say. She only knew her instinct almost screamed at the idea.

'Well,' Sam said slowly, 'maybe at that it would make a more interesting story if Jeb takes her by surprise.' He glanced at Ben with a wry face. 'I'd like to see his face, too ... he and his daddy don't get on, I'm told, and the way he's been pursuing Clea this past week makes one wonder. I'd say he came here with the set intention of getting her into bed to spite his daddy.'

'You sadist!' Joanne muttered harshly, her face draining of colour.

'Oh, come on,' shrugged Sam, unconcerned. 'It's my job to speculate on what the famous are up to, remember.'

'Famous last words,' she snapped. 'Anyone who does a rotten job claims that.'

'I'm as necessary to Clea as her make-up man,' Sam said half angrily. 'She needs me as much as I need her. The day I stop taking an interest in her private life will be a black day in her book.'

Joanne knew very well that he was right, but she was angry with him. There had been a ring of personal amusement in the way he spoke about Ben, and she resented it.

'Lester has asked Ben to invest in Clea's new film,' she said defensively, 'that's all.' She might be giving away information to Sam by telling him about the film, but it was better than having him speculate so damningly about Ben's relationship with Clea.

Sam lifted one eyebrow. 'The film nobody wants to back?'

Joanne went cold. 'What?' Her voice was hoarse.

'Come on,' said Sam, smiling. 'It's a fairly open

secret. Clea's last film didn't have the box office pull the film backers like, so they've all steered clear of investing any more money in her.'

'That isn't true!' Joanne stared at him, apprehensively, her skin pale and cold. Was it true? There had been something odd going on for weeks, a touch of quiet distress about Milly's face whenever she looked at Clea, a touch of edgy anxiety about Clea from time to time. Joanne knew that the two of them had secrets from her. They were so close, and she had never been involved in the business side of things.

Sam watched her face drily. 'Sweetie, it's been clear for some time that the skids are under Clea.'

'No,' she protested, shivering.

'What do you think made her so mad in that last interview? I asked her about the rumour that her last film hadn't made enough money and she upped and chucked a glass of Martini in my face.' His eyes hardened. 'I didn't like that, darling. I didn't like it at all.'

She said huskily, 'I'm sorry, Sam ... she must have been upset.'

'She upset me,' he said, the trace of menace in his voice deepening.

She had to soothe him down. She could not let him hurt Clea. Or Ben, she thought, shuddering.

'Don't be cross,' she pleaded, smiling at him placatingly.

His eyes narrowed, slid down her slender body in the flame dress. 'Come out into the garden and apologise there,' he said softly.

It was a blatant piece of blackmail, but she was afraid of what Sam could do, she was terrified that he would walk up to Clea publicly and say something which could wound her intolerably. Clea was more vulnerable than she had known. She had been unaware of the pressures building up and tonight she had increased them with her little flare of rebellion. She knew how terrified of growing old Clea was, she should not have done it.

'If that's what you want,' she said, moving off the floor.

As they went through the terrace doors, Sam paused, 'I'll get us some champagne,' he said. 'To put us in a party mood.'

She walked out alone into the warm, dark night and looked up at the crescent moon, hung like a silver boat, against a backcloth of gently drifting clouds. The air was warm on her skin. The trees in Lester's garden whispered in the faint wind.

'I hope you know what you're doing,' murmured a voice behind her, and she swung round, heart thudding.

'What do you mean?'

'Come off it,' he said curtly. 'Sam Ransom is a shark. You're too young to get bitten.'

'I'm not a fool,' she said, her eyes angry.

'Aren't you?' His mouth was ironic. The wind blew her black hair crazily, strands of it flung across his face. She put up a hand to brush it down and touched his skin, feeling the brief contact like hot iron on her palm. Involuntarily she jerked away, and he looked at her sharply.

'What's the matter?'

'Nothing,' she whispered huskily, shaking.

He stared at her for a silent moment, then his hands closed over her shoulders and he drew her against his body. There was a peculiar fixity in them both. Joanne swallowed, her heart pounding. Ben stared down at her. His head began to bend slowly, his hands tightened on her shoulders. She knew he was going to kiss her, and for a second her mouth lifted hungrily for the touch of his, then she pulled away, a hot anger inside her.

'I'm not my mother,' she muttered through her teeth. 'And I'm not her stand-in, either.'

She saw the dark colour rise in his face. 'You little bitch,' he muttered, shaking her with hands that hurt.

Sam's footsteps broke into the intensity which was holding them both. Ben gave her one savage look and almost flung her away, turned on his heel and stalked off, passing Sam with a black look.

'What,' asked Sam softly, 'was all that about?'

'Nothing,' she said, assuming a wild gaiety. 'Where's my champagne, Sam? I thought this was a party?'

He eyed her curiously. 'Here you are, princess,' he said, handing her a glass and took a sip from his own, his eyes on her flushed face. 'You're looking very passionate.'

She drained her glass with a reckless smile. 'Is that bad?'

Sam put his glass down and took her in his arms. 'No, sweetheart, very good,' he said softly, and his mouth closed over her own before she had notice of his intention.

For a second she almost cried aloud in misery and protest. Her first kiss ... and it could have been Ben, she thought! Why had she stopped him? Oh, God, I'm a fool, she thought. What difference did it make that her first kiss should come from Sam Ransom instead of Ben Norris? Neither of them meant anything to her or she to them.

They stayed out there for twenty minutes. She let him kiss her, indeed she invited it, her smile as beguiling as she could make it. She put her arms round his neck, kissing him back, but there was no excitement in the exchanged embrace. She tried hard, but just the memory of Ben's mouth coming down towards hers could make her heart beat until she felt she would be sick, and Sam's experienced kisses could not erase the memory.

'I get the feeling I'm kissing a statue,' Sam said wryly, his eyes studying her. 'All the passion I saw in your face when Ben Norris was out here has vanished.'

She lifted her head, the black hair flowing in the wind, and gave him a secret look from under her lashes. 'Promise to be nice to my mother?'

'What is this? Who's blackmailing who?' he asked teasingly, and she moved her fingers into his ruffled hair, smiling at him, leaning back from the waist, her body casually touching him.

'We're blackmailing each other,' she said, then leant forward and slowly kissed him with real feeling, hating herself because she was pretending and she knew it, pretending he was someone else.

Sam pushed her away, his hands hard on her waist. 'How much champagne have you drunk, darling?' His eyes were strangely cold. 'I'm beginning to do some sums, I warn you.'

Sam was shrewd and clever. He might well do

accurate mathematics, and she glared at him. 'You asked me out here.'

'All right,' he said flatly. 'I got what I asked for and I wish to hell I'd known better. No man likes to stand in for another feller, darling ... even if he's blackmailed a girl into kissing him.' He took her arm and pushed her towards the door. 'Consider the debt cancelled,' he said. 'I'll treat Clea like china—and from now on, Joanne, stay out of my path.'

She was puzzled by his anger. He had wanted to make love to her and he had—why was he so annoyed now? He had known from the start that she was not out here with him from choice.

Ben was facing the terrace doors, talking to Lester, and the dark eyes registered their entrance and, she knew, comprehended some of what had happened outside. His hard mouth twisted in a sardonic, pointed smile and she looked through him as though he were invisible, her hand tightening on Sam's arm.

He looked down at her, eyes narrowed. 'My God, Joanne, don't be a fool,' he muttered almost angrily. 'Clea would kill you if you went after him...'

'I wouldn't have him as a present,' she said fiercely.

Sam almost smiled. 'You'd never make an actress,' he said. 'You can't lie for toffee.'

Clea came drifting over to them, against the black silk her skin gleamed like pearl, lustrous and delicate. She looked at Joanne briefly, then at Sam with a raised eyebrow. 'Now, what have you been doing in the garden with my daughter, Sam?' The question was sharp.

'Kissing her madly,' Sam said so mockingly that Clea did not believe him, but Ben, coming up behind her, overheard, and he did, his dark eyes told Joanne so with cold malice.

Clea had not really come over to cross-question Sam. She moved on to the real reason for her joining them. 'Ben has agreed to back my film, darlings,' she said gaily, including them both in her smile. 'So as soon as everything is signed we're off to the States.'

'How exciting,' Sam said drily, looking at Ben's impassive face. Joanne waited with tension for him to add something biting, but he looked down at her with an odd expression and said nothing more.

Clea was looking very beautiful, her excitement making her shine and sparkle. She kissed Joanne's cold cheek, saying, 'How cold your face is, darling ... you shouldn't have stayed out in the garden for so long.'

Ben stared at Joanne icily. 'She was enjoying herself,' he said, and he meant it to sting.

'Yes,' she said sweetly, 'I was.'

Suddenly the room fell silent and everyone seemed to turn and stare at them. Aware of the tension, Clea glanced around and Joanne looked, too, puzzled. A man was coming across the room towards them and one look told her who he was, the resemblance was striking.

He stooped slightly, as though he spent much of his day at a desk, but his features were toughened by assurance and years of power and he bore the stamp of a man accustomed to getting his own way. His hair was dusted with silver, his eyes surrounded with lines, his skin tanned to a leather-like shade and texture. There was faint humour in the dark eyes, in the line of the mouth, but at this moment she could not read the expression on his face. He was staring at Clea and she was staring back, as if she was oblivious of all the watching eyes, her face white and stricken, her body tense.

Miserably, Joanne looked at Ben. How would he take the appearance of his father at this moment?

CHAPTER THREE

SHE had no difficulty in reading the expression on that hard face. He was as taken aback as she was by his father's appearance, and clearly not pleased. The dark eyes were narrowed in a stare which sent her heart sinking to her stomach.

She looked quickly again at Clea, then back at Ben, and instinctively caught hold of his arm, holding him back as Clea moved slowly to meet Jeb alone.

He turned towards her, his face grim.

'Leave them alone,' she said in a low voice. She was breathless, as though she had run a mile, and her heart was thumping against her breastbone, so that she wondered if her anxiety was visible.

For a second she thought he would hit her. His face was congested with dark blood, his eyes brilliantly black. Her fingers tightened around his arm, digging into him, and he looked down at her as if she were an intrusive insect he would brush off with a flick of his finger.

'What are you? Her bodyguard?' The words were delivered in a quiet, sneering tone which made her shrink, but she kept hold of him.

'Everyone is staring,' she whispered back. 'Stay out of it!'

He lifted his head and shot a look around the room. She had not exaggerated. Everyone was wildly excited by the real-life drama going on under their noses, hardly knowing which of them to watch, their eyes shooting from Clea and Jeb Norris, and then to his son. Ben had been Clea's constant companion for the past week and people were dying of curiosity to see how he would re-act to his father's sudden arrival.

Joanne glanced at Sam Ransom and his eye caught the movement of her head. He turned his own and stared at her unreadably. She knew that the little scene being played out was meat and drink to him, but she was determined that he should not have a chance to crucify Ben in his gossip column next day.

'Come outside,' she whispered to Ben, pulling at his wrist. He looked down at her with cold eyes, but allowed her to pull him out into the garden.

Outside she released him and he turned in the shadows to watch the drama in the centre of the lighted room. From out here it was like sitting in the audi-torium watching a scene on a brilliantly lit stage. Jeb Norris stood in front of Clea and looked down at her. She was very still, her eyes lifted to his face. Her hands hung at her sides, their fingers curled, as though she were a little girl brought before the headmaster for some misdeed.

Clea's mouth trembled visibly. She said something inaudible, and Joanne winced at the expression in her mother's eyes, astonished by it. Clea seemed to beg, the black lashes quivering, and Jeb Norris's face was totally enigmatic, his features fully under control.

In the silence the music from the other room hung hauntingly like an echo.

Ben swore under his breath, his hands clenched. Joanne shot him a worried look. Was he in love with Clea? She felt suddenly that she had to get him away from the scene, she had to get his attention. 'Come and look at the rose terrace,' she said. 'It can be very impressive in the moonlight.'

He hardly seemed to hear her. She took his arm firmly and he looked down at her with a start. She repeated her words and he smiled, a cold movement of his mouth without humour or warmth.

'Why not?' he asked between his teeth.

They walked down the path and emerged on the terrace. Clea had designed it for Lester some years ago. The grey stone walls and paths fell one after the other with beds of roses sandwiched between them. The terrace looked its best on a summer morning when the colours and scents of the flowers were embellished by the sun, but in moonlight it took on a gentle, haunted quality, the roses drained of their colour, ghostly, yet still leaving that soft, warm fragrance on the night air, retaining the imprint of sunshine on their petals.

The heady sweetness filled their nostrils. Joanne inhaled, leaned on a stone post which formed a gateway. 'Lovely, isn't it?'

He threw a look around him which barely seemed to take in anything of the scene. 'Lovely,' he said curtly, not meaning a word of it, and she saw his head turn back towards the house.

'Stay here!'

He gave her a sardonic stare. 'What do you imagine I'm going to do? Burst into tears or play a jealous scene in front of everyone?'

'Are you in love with her?' The question burst out involuntarily and she felt colour burning in her face as if the question were a bitter accusation.

He laughed, his mouth sneering. 'My God, she's the last woman in the world I could ever fall for! She made my childhood hell on earth.'

The reply startled her. Her eyes flew open to their fullest. 'But ... you were going to back her film...'

'Was I?' His mouth twisted.

'She just told us you were.' Joanne stared at him, baffled. 'I don't understand...'

'Oh, hell,' he said thickly, turning away and walking down the steps among the clustering rose bushes.

She followed slowly, frowning, watching the lean dark figure move with worried eyes. At the base of the terrace there was a stone-walled fish pond, the moonlit surface thick with lily pads. Ben sat on the wall and ruffled the water with one careless hand.

She joined him and sat down, her own eyes on the water. The moon slid behind a cloud and the garden lay in darkness for a moment, then it came out again and she saw its pale reflection shine on the dark surface.

'I knew all about her while I was at boarding school,' he said, as if talking to himself, his voice conversational. 'One of the boys showed me a story in a newspaper. The boys were all gloating over it. Boys can be sadistic little animals. There was a picture of her—she looked like Helen of Troy. When I went home next holidays my mother had begun to drink. When she was drunk she talked ... God, how she talked! She told me all about it. She had always drunk quite a bit, but my father's affair with Clea Thorpe had speeded up the process.'

Joanne watched his dark profile with compassion, imagining the little boy abruptly disillusioned about his parents, shown the chasm between them in this cruel fashion, aware of the brittle nature of their marriage, and afraid for his own security. Poor little boy, she thought. She could imagine him; seven years old, in short school trousers, his face defenceless and aggressive, trying to hide his uncertainty behind a tough exterior.

'My mother's drinking got so bad she had to go away,' he went on in that distant, hard voice. 'She would come home for a while and seem cured, but eventually it would all start again, and she would go again. My father said it was an illness, and I suppose it was, but I hated it ... I hated her. I hated my father. I despised them both.'

She remembered him as she first saw him, framed in the doorway at her mother's party, a cold, contemptuous stranger. What he was telling her explained the sardonic mockery, the remote coldness.

But why had he come to Clea's party that night? Why had he gone on seeing her, dining out with her night after night, haunting the villa, flattering and flirting with her?

'Women like Clea should be forced to wear a mask,' he said. 'She's like Medusa ... she has a disastrous effect on the men who look at her.'

'She hardly turns them to stone,' said Joanne, trying for a light tone, and his eyes cut her like knives.

'She destroys them,' he said, his mouth implacable.

She shivered.

'You never saw my mother,' he said. 'Before she died she looked like a ruined house, empty, shattered. My father told me she was pretty when she was young.'

'You can't blame Clea for what happened to your mother!'

He stared at her with those icy eyes. 'Can't I?'

'You have no right to judge her!'

'What gives her the right to use her looks as a searchlight, trapping men like moths?'

Joanne thought of the moment when he met Clea, the nervous, uncertain way her mother had looked at him, and his expression of incredulous admiration. Clea had done nothing to bring about that look. She had merely stood there, waiting, like some blind goddess, and Ben had crashed to his knees.

'She doesn't do it deliberately,' she protested. 'It just happens.'

He laughed bitterly. 'Does it?'

'I've seen it happening,' she said. 'Do you think you were the first man to cave in at the sight of her?'

His eyes flashed. 'Cave in?' he repeated, then he laughed oddly. 'And now my father is getting the treatment, is he? So you brought me out here to keep me out of the way while she worked on him?'

She flushed, glancing away, and his hand curved around her chin, lifting her face so that the moonlight illuminated it, giving her eyes a pale glitter and touching her mouth with sweetness.

'Do you work as a pair?' he asked unpleasantly.

'What?' She was bewildered, her face frowning.

'That was why you brought Sam Ransom out here, wasn't it? To sweeten him and stop him writing something damaging about Clea?'

His insight made her start, her eyes widening then quickly dropping from his face, her lids hiding the expression from him.

'Clever stuff,' he drawled. 'Those Clea can't handle get passed on to you, do they? You're an impressive team. My God, I had you down wrongly. The first time I saw you, I barely noticed you.'

She had been aware of that, resenting it, and her quick upward look told him so.

He gave her a bitter smile. 'You were such an innocent-looking kid, no make-up, straight hair, big blue eyes ... I was even sorry for you at times. What a house to be brought up in, I thought ... poor kid! You puzzled me, though. Now and then I caught a flash of something which didn't fit.' His eyes slowly ran down her body in the flame dress and she shivered under that stare. 'Then tonight I saw you dancing with Ransom in that ... and the mask was off. You were giving him the treatment, weren't you? Sweet come-hither smiles, seductive looks ... I watched you and I could have kicked myself for being such a blind fool.'

He was still holding her chin and she tried to pull back, her mouth trembling.

'Let me go,' she whispered shakily.

'Why should I?' His hand tightened, then slid to her throat, making her shiver at the unexpectedly sensual impact of his fingers on her cool skin. His eyes glinted at her, mockery in their depths. 'Why are you trembling?'

'I'm angry,' she snapped. 'I don't like being manhandled.'

'No?' His mouth twisted. 'Tell that to the Marines! I suppose you and Ransom were star-spotting while you were out here for half an hour?'

'That's none of your business!'

He laughed. 'Oh, I don't give a damn ... it was revealing, though. It showed me just how you and your damned mother played your little game.' He stared down at her, his eyes unreadable in the moonlight. 'I'm sorry if it isn't going the way you expected,' he mocked. 'But never mind ... you might as well give me what you brought me out here for.'

Before she could move his mouth came down, brushing against her lips lightly, cool from the night air, making her tense and quiver. She had wanted him so badly to kiss her and now she shrank from it, putting her hands up to his shoulders to push him away, twisting and turning to evade his mouth.

He was immovable, his fingers bruising the soft skin of her throat as they tightened, holding her in his power.

'Don't,' she whispered miserably. He was hurting her intolerably. Pain was stabbing inside her as every word he had said repeated in her mind. He hated and despised her. The soft kisses he was giving her were poisoned with his contempt.

'What's the matter?' he asked mockingly. 'Have I spoilt your act? Come on, sweetheart, give me what you gave Ransom.'

She started to protest angrily, but his lips silenced her, hardening and possessing until he had forced her mouth to part. His hands moved from her throat and slid down her back, bending her as if she were a doll. Joanne clutched at his shoulders in an effort to retain her balance, and the compelling movement of his mouth awoke a hunger in her. She lost the capacity to think. She was all feeling, her body responding in restless passion, her hands reaching for him, clinging to him.

She felt him draw a long breath. His hands drew her closer, his mouth burned on her own and she yielded mindlessly, kissing him back with a passion which was rapidly passing into delirium. Her fingers crept into his hair, wound into the thick strands, holding his head as if to keep it in her control, pulling it down towards her. When Sam Ransom kissed her she had forced herself to stand still in his arms, hating it, but now she was on fire, melting like wax, feeling the erotic caress of Ben's hands over her body with every nerve.

He suddenly thrust her away, breathing as though he had been running. 'You're your mother's daughter all right,' he said in a barbed sneer.

After the exchanged passion it was like a douche of cold water in her face. Joanne shook, trying to control the pain. When her voice seemed steady, she said huskily, 'What did you expect? Snow White?'

'God knows,' he muttered, turning to walk away. She stayed where she was, shivering, drained and miserable. She forced herself to stare at the moonlit water as if her life depended on it. If I'm not careful, she thought, I shall fall in love with him and that would be a recipe for disaster. There is nothing but pain in loving him.

She did not understand what had brought him here, why he had pursued Clea so openly, why he had promised to back her new film, but one thing she was certain about—he hated both of them. His tone, his face, his words had convinced her of that.

As a child she had loved Clea with all her heart, hardly sparing any affection for her father or anyone else. She had grown up seeing Clea at close quarters, recognising the feet of clay all idols possess yet still loving her because Clea was her mother, and had qualities beside the heartlessness towards men, the shallowness of emotion. She could be kind, thoughtful, easy-tempered. Joanne had never grown out of her love for her mother, but she was increasingly realising that living with Clea was dangerous to herself. While she lived in the shadow of that great beauty, that fame, that magic, she was unable to become herself.

I have to get away, she thought. I have to leave the shadows before I become a shadow myself. The Lady of Shalott had to leave her loom, even though she knew the curse would come upon her, because a life lived safely in shadowed seclusion is no life at all.

She went back into the party later. Clea was with Jeb Norris in one corner of the room. She was unusually silent, listening as he spoke to her, her violet eyes on his face, and he was speaking softly, his head bent towards her, watching her.

Ben was drinking with a concentrated intensity which worried her, his glance on the other two, but there was nothing in that hard, dark face to give her a clue as to his intentions.

'We're going, darling,' Clea said ten minutes later, smiling at her. Jeb Norris stood at her side, his hand beneath her elbow, and Joanne looked into his face searchingly, receiving a quiet smile from him.

'So you're Joanne,' he said, as if he was pleased with her, as if she matched up to his idea of Clea's daughter, and although she was sick and miserable at that moment a faint warmth reached her from him, and she smiled at him.

'Yes,' she said, and he smiled back.

He took the driver's seat as if by right and Clea accepted it without comment, sitting beside him submissively, staring out at the unrolling road. Joanne had the feeling that she was wrapped in happiness. She had never seen her look so calm, and she remembered what Milly had said about Clea caring more for Jeb than any other man who had ever come into her life.

When they arrived Joanne said 'Goodnight,' with a pleasant smile, turning towards the stairs, and Jeb Norris halted her with a hand on her arm. 'Sleep well, Joanne,' he said quietly. 'I'll look forward to getting to know you.'

She liked him; it was instinctive. But she was worried and she stood in her own room staring out of the window at the moonwashed garden with a feeling of unease.

Had Jeb Norris come to rescue Clea from his son, or his son from Clea? It could not be coincidence which brought him here so opportunely. Clea was so happy and Joanne felt like someone watching a tragedy they were powerless to halt.

She could not sleep, tortured by memories of those

moments in the rose garden with Ben. He had kissed her out of anger and hatred, and she wished violently that she had not enjoyed being in his arms, but she had to admit she had. She had been waiting for it ever since she met him. She had yearned to know how it would feel to have him kiss her. Now she knew, and it was shame and delight. He had not kissed her because he wanted to—he had been punishing her because of her mother. He had despised her, condemned her unjustly, his kisses had been an insult, and she had to despise herself for responding with such passion.

When at last she undressed and got into bed she lay awake for a long time, her mind in turmoil, but at last she fell into a troubled sleep and awoke at first light feeling grey and listless.

She showered and dressed in white jeans and a blue shirt, then whistled to Harry and took him down the cliff path in the softening light, hearing the birds begin their morning chorus in the trees above her and the sound of the sea coming gently up the cliff towards them.

She was not surprised to see Ben walking on the beach, but her nerves tightened painfully. She would have gone back, but he turned his head and looked at her with those cold dark eyes and pride made her lift her head and walk forward without a sign of uneasiness.

Harry leapt around him eagerly, panting. Ben threw a stick for him and they both watched silently as the dog tore after it into the sea.

'Sleep well, did you?' Ben asked, and his tone cut her.

She flushed. 'Thank you. Did you?'

He turned those sardonic eyes on her and she clenched her hands at her side, knowing that he had not been to bed at all. She had the feeling he had been walking here all night, thinking, planning—but what? She got no clue from that stony countenance. He might have been a marble statue, except for the bitter coldness in those dark eyes.

'I'm going to Paris for a few days,' he said expressionlessly.

Her heart sank. 'Oh?' she said, hoping her misery at the news did not reach him.

He stared at her, face unreadable. 'Come with me.'

Colour ran up her face. 'No!' she said hotly, hating him.

He lifted one thin eyebrow. 'What can I promise that will persuade you? How much will it cost? A diamond bracelet like your mother's? A fur coat?'

She turned to run away and his hand descended on her arm, halting her forcibly.

'Let go of me!'

Ben watched as she struggled impotently, her face scarlet with insulted anger, and his own face was as cool as iced water.

'I want you,' he said. 'And I'll pay for it. I know these things cost money.'

Her hand swung up and he caught it, his fingers vice-like around her wrist. 'Oh, no, you don't, darling,' he drawled. 'We both know the score. I may be presenting it badly, but don't pretend it's something you've never done before.'

She was so unhappy, so angry, that her eyes rose to

his face and she said in a choked voice, 'You're wrong! I ... I've never ...' The words jammed together in her throat and refused to emerge, but her frantic miserable eyes spoke for her and he stared at her, brows pulling together.

His eyes ran down over her slender body in the simple jeans and shirt, came back to her clear-skinned face, innocent of cosmetics, her straight hair and angry eyes.

'Do you expect me to believe that you're the innocent you look?'

'No,' she said bitterly. 'I don't expect you to believe anything, but it's the truth, whether you believe it or not.'

'Promises but no deliveries,' he muttered, and she winced. His eyes swept over her again, narrowed and strangely sharp. 'At least your mother delivers. My father didn't come back last night, did he?'

The colour drained from her face. 'I've no idea,' she said huskily.

He laughed. 'Of course not. My God, you and your mother are a great team!'

'Don't insult my mother,' she said furiously.

'Your mother is a ...'

She pulled her hand from his wrist with a violent movement and hit him before the word emerged, and he swore, grabbing both her arms and holding her immobile between his hands.

'Can't you take the truth? What would you call her? And what do you call yourself? What did you offer Sam Ransom to soothe him down last night? And me later? You were promising whatever I wanted and you know it ... a cold-blooded little tease, Joanne, that's what you are.'

She was suddenly weary, her eyes lowered, close to tears. 'Please let me go, Ben.'

There was a silence, then he released her and she turned away, with Harry capering around her, stick in mouth. She walked away stiffly and Ben watched her with his hands driven into his pockets. She hoped she would never set eyes on him again. He had hurt her enough to last a lifetime. She could not take any more pain.

She swam for an hour because she felt unclean and the cool brush of the water on her overheated body was soothing, washing away some of the misery Ben had inflicted on her.

He had wanted to humiliate her and he had succeeded, beyond his knowledge, because he was not aware how much she cared. She refused to admit even to herself how much she cared. She steered her thoughts carefully away from it whenever they came too close.

When she came back into the house Jeb Norris was standing in the drawing-room staring at the great portrait of Clea hanging over the fireplace. It had been painted when Joanne was two. She did not remember it, but she remembered the painting from her earliest years, having spent hours staring at it with silent awe. Her mother's beauty at that age had been unbelievable and the artist had captured it for ever with great skill.

The blue eyes held a sweet, haunted smile. The

mouth was tender, exquisite. The translucent glow of the skin was almost touchable, one could have sworn that if one laid a hand on it one would feel the blood move beneath the skin.

Jeb turned and looked at her wryly. 'She was the loveliest thing I ever saw,' he said, and his voice was sad.

'She still is,' Joanne said too quickly, and their eyes held in a moment of exchanged knowledge.

'You're not a child,' said Jeb. 'You will have heard something about me. Old myths have a way of changing, being embellished. I want you to know that I loved your mother.'

Joanne noted the past tense with slight anxiety. She walked over and joined him and looked at him searchingly. 'Why have you come, Mr Norris?'

He smiled. 'You're very straightforward, Joanne. I like that.' He looked at the picture and sighed. 'The answer is complicated. Firstly I came because I've been reading highly coloured gossip items about Clea and my son ...'

Joanne's breathing tightened and he looked at her sharply.

'How often has Ben been here?'

'Quite often during the last week,' she said expressionlessly.

He nodded. 'So it was true.'

'You haven't asked Clea?'

He laughed. 'Would she tell me the truth?' His brows registered wry amusement. 'Clea is very lovely, but she tells lies when she thinks it's necessary.'

Joanne flushed, looking away. 'Please don't!' She

could not listen to any more brutal remarks about her mother. She would not listen.

Jeb Norris watched her thoughtfully. 'Nobody is perfect, Joanne,' he said. 'I love Clea just the way she is.'

This time it was the present tense, and her eyes flew to his face. 'Love?' she repeated huskily.

'Yes,' he said frankly. 'I said the answer was complicated—it is. When I read that Ben had been seeing Clea I was knocked sideways. It seemed almost incestuous.' He grinned at her. 'I haven't seen her since she ran off with your father, but I still thought of her possessively. Once I realised that, I knew I had to come here ... I knew I still loved her.'

She sighed, her shoulders relaxing from the tension which had held them.

'What has Ben been up to?' he asked her, watching her.

'Hadn't you better ask him that?'

'I doubt if he'd be frank,' Jeb said ruefully. 'He and I have barely spoken to each other for years. He can't stand the sight of me. The blood rushed to my head when I heard he'd been seeing Clea because I had a shrewd idea he was getting back at me through her, and I still think that was his plan.'

Perhaps it had been, she thought. Ben had come here to hurt if he could, but had he been untouched by Clea's loveliness or had he been as bowled over by it as most other men were?

'Clea says he was going to back her new film.' Jeb stared down at her, lifting an eyebrow quizzically. 'Do you think that's the case?'

'That's what they both told me,' she said, but Ben

had said later 'Was I?' in a biting tone which made it impossible to guess what he really meant to do.

'I can see why that appealed to Clea,' Jeb murmured. 'But what was Ben up to? He hates her. What was he playing at?'

He hates her. Joanne shivered. Yes, Ben hated Clea and he hated her, too, as Clea's daughter. He despised them both. What had he been planning? Had he meant to let Clea get excited about the film, feel safe and happy again, only to let her down publicly, drop the film and her with it? That would have humiliated Clea. It would have hurt. It might even have ended her film career if she could not find another backer.

'I'm going to marry her,' said Jeb, and she looked at him in surprise. 'I want her tied up so tight she'll never get away from me again.' He grinned, ruefully self-mocking. 'She got away from me once. Never again.'

Joanne laughed. 'Have you told her?'

'Yes,' said Jeb, and his eyes were hard. 'I told her.'

Clea was not getting a man who would run after her like a pet dog this time. She was getting a man who for all his amused affection for her was granite at bottom, and looking at him, Joanne could see where Ben got it from, that stony, unmoving expression.

'God help her if she plays me up,' Jeb added, and he was not being funny. Joanne could see that. How would Clea cope with him? she wondered. She was spoilt, hopelessly spoilt by years of getting her own way and now she would find herself being managed firmly but inexorably and how would she like that?

'Have you seen Ben since you arrived?' she asked him anxiously.

He shook his head. 'You know, Ben had a bad childhood. His mother was a sick woman.'

'He told me,' she said miserably.

He looked at her sharply. 'He did? That's interesting. He rarely talks about her. It was hard for him—young boys are sensitive. She was his mother, yet he despised her. He showed it openly and it hurt her. He looked at her, talked to her, with contempt. I had to talk to him about it, and we had some bad rows. When he got older he changed towards her ... he started taking her side, protecting her, as he saw it, against me.' His mouth twisted. 'Ben despised me. He knew all about Clea, of course.' He laughed harshly. 'One thing about Ben ... he never had women trouble.'

Joanne could believe that. Ben would hate and despise women. Her first impression of him had been accurate. The cold, sardonic stranger looking around that room full of beautiful women, dismissing them all with contempt, had been Ben's true persona.

They had both been born outsiders. She had hidden in the shadows, effacing herself, while Ben had turned to face the rest of the world, deliberately isolating himself and despising everyone he met.

'He couldn't blame me more than I blamed myself,' Jeb told her. 'I'd stopped loving my wife before I met Clea. Linda had a cancer of the mind. Her drinking had nothing to do with Clea, but Ben would never have believed that. It didn't start when I met Clea. It had been kept out of sight, but it was there long before that. Linda tried to stop it, but she couldn't and that was what killed my feelings for her, not Clea.'

Joanne was embarrassed, not wishing to hear all this, because it was involving her more and more with Ben, making her see far too clearly how terrible his life must have been as a child.

'Please,' she muttered miserably, and Jeb looked at her with a grimace.

'I'm sorry, I shouldn't have told you all this ... it's none of your business. I've embarrassed you.' He patted her shoulder, smiling. 'I'm taking Clea to lunch in Nice. I'd like to take you, too.'

She smiled back politely. 'Thank you, but I have another date. Some other time, I hope.'

'You can be sure of that,' he said firmly. 'I want to get to know you, Joanne. How do you feel about me as a stepfather?'

She laughed. 'I think it might be fun!'

He looked delighted. 'I promise it will be,' he said, nodding. 'I've always wanted a daughter to spoil and fuss over ... nobody was allowed to fuss over Ben. He was a very stubborn, difficult boy.'

Boy, she thought wryly. Had he ever been that? The word did not apply to that hard, dark arrogant face and she could not think of him except as the man whose touch last night had turned her bones to water and made her heart beat like a drum.

Clea came in looking ravishing in a simple blue dress, the skirt full, the bodice cut low and suspended on thin straps which crossed over her throat. A white bolero covered her bare shoulders. She looked barely older than Joanne and Jeb smiled at her in admiration.

When she looked up at him the little-girl look was

in her eyes and her mouth was sweetly submissive. Jeb kissed her and Clea looked radiant as she drew back from him.

She gave Joanne a little, shy smile, her eyes searching to catch her daughter's reaction. Joanne smiled back at her because Clea looked so vulnerable, so uncertain.

'I would have loved to come with you, but I have another appointment,' she said, and Clea looked at Jeb.

'What a pity,' she said.

'We have plenty of time for Joanne and me to get to know each other,' he said.

'And Milly,' Clea put in quickly.

He smiled at her. 'Don't worry, Clea. You won't lose a thing by marrying me. Milly and Joanne will come with us.'

Clea looked at Joanne to see how she reacted to the idea of the marriage and Joanne nodded reassuringly. Jeb took her off and Milly stood with Joanne in the window watching them drive away.

'Jeb Norris was always a man to reckon with,' Milly said with bland satisfaction. 'This time he will marry her.'

'You'll stay?' Joanne asked, and Milly gave her an offended look.

'Do you think wild horses would drag me away from Clea?'

'No,' said Joanne, laughing. 'And I don't think Clea would let anyone part her from you, either.' She looked away and said quietly, 'But I'm not coming. I'm going to England.'

Milly stiffened, staring. 'Why? Jeb?'

'No, but I think it's time I got to know my father,' Joanne explained. 'I've never spent any time over there with him. Now Clea will have Jeb and I can go without feeling guilty.'

Something in Milly's probing stare told her that Milly was not convinced by her reasoning but Milly said nothing much, except to sigh. 'You know your mind best.'

CHAPTER FOUR

JOANNE could not settle to anything that afternoon. She and Milly ate a simple salad lunch, then Milly went off to work in the study and Joanne whistled to Harry, but he was languid in the afternoon heat and showed no inclination to move from his shady place in the garden, so she walked off alone. She had tied her long hair up in a ponytail and wore her jeans and a clean blue shirt, gingham, giving her a neat, schoolgirlish look.

There were a number of people on the beach. She avoided them, strolling through the sand, scuffling it with her sandalled feet, her head bent. When she came down to the water she took off her sandals and walked through it, her jeans rolled up, kicking the waves with her toes, her sandals in her hands.

A motorboat came perilously close and she looked round, startled. Ben was driving it, his shoulders glistening with sea spray, wearing only swimming briefs. 'Come for a ride,' he shouted above the sound of the engine, and she shook her head, turning away.

The boat swerved in and the engine cut. He leaned

on the side as it drifted some feet away from her. 'I'm sorry about my foul temper this morning and last night,' he said.

She looked at him then, flushing. 'Forget it,' she said flatly.

'Forgive me?' he asked, and she looked away, nodding without reply.

She would never forgive him, but what was the point of saying so?

'Then come for a ride,' he said.

She shook her head, wishing he would go away. Some boys playing with a ball threw it and it bobbed on the water brightly. Ben leaned over and grasped it, threw it back, his body moving gracefully, the lithe brown chest glistening with salt. She looked at him and her mouth went dry.

He turned the black head and their eyes met. 'I don't usually behave like a swine,' he said.

'Don't you?' She could not stop the retort.

'Ouch!' he said wryly. 'I deserved that.' His black hair blew in the wind, tousled and untidy, and there was a fine trail of black hairs leading down his chest to where the black line of the briefs began. 'What else have you got to do?' he asked conversationally. 'Come on, Joanne ... I leave for Paris tomorrow.'

She halted, head bent, and he leaned over the side and caught her wrist, pulling her through the water towards him. She struggled without conviction and in a moment found him hauling her over the side. The engine started up again and the boat roared away out to sea. She scrambled upright on to the seat beside him.

'Take me back, Ben.'

He didn't answer, staring through the windshield at the flying spray and the white-topped waves. They seemed to be flying on top of the sea. It flew up on either side in churned drops, dampening her shirt, flicking her cheeks with coldness.

There was no point in arguing with him; he had to take her back some time. She sat back staring out at the hazy sea. The afternoon sun lay like a red ball in the drifting mists on the horizon. Some gulls were playing tag overhead, screaming with gaping mouths.

A large yacht appeared ahead of them and she glanced at it without much interest. It did not appear to be going anywhere. It was stationary in the blue sea, rocking gently on the water.

Ben zoomed alongside it and the engine cut. She looked at him in surprise. 'Up you go,' he said, his hands hard on her waist, lifting her.

'What do you think you're doing?' She was taken aback, baffled. 'Whose yacht is it?'

'A friend of mine,' he said. 'We'll have tea with him.'

'But...'

'Go on,' he said curtly, pushing her, and she placed her feet in the ladder, finding the rungs with difficulty as the yacht moved to and fro. A man appeared at the top of the ladder and hauled her aboard. She straightened, gasping, and he grinned at her, his black eyes slipping down over her.

'Hello,' Joanne said in English, and when his face remained blank repeated it in French. Ben reached the deck behind her and said softly, 'He's Greek ... he doesn't speak English or French. Do you speak Greek?'

'No,' she said, smiling at the man, who cheerfully

beamed back. He was very short, very brown and had thick black curly hair. He was wearing a T-shirt and brief shorts.

'Is he your friend?' It would be a strange tea party, she thought, if they could not communicate.

Ben laughed. 'No, he's one of the crew.' He turned his head and spoke in swift Greek and the man laughed, looking strangely at Joanna.

'What did you say to him?' she asked suspiciously.

'I told him we'd come for tea,' he said, straight-faced. He took her hand and led her to some stairs, gesturing for her to go down them. She found herself facing some doors. Ben leapt past and opened one, pushed her slightly so that she went into the cabin. She halted, seeing that not only was it unoccupied but that it was a bedroom. Ben was behind her and as she turned, panic-stricken, he locked the door and retained the key, leaning his back on it with a mocking smile.

She whitened. 'Let me out, Ben!'

He strolled past her and threw himself on the bed, lounging back casually, his hands behind his head. 'Come here.'

'Ben, I want to go home.'

'I'm in no hurry,' he said, his hard mouth smiling coldly. 'I can wait.'

She turned and hammered on the door, shouting in English and French. 'Help ... *aidez moi*! Please let me out ... *ouvrez la porte*!'

'There's only Nico on board,' Ben said. 'And he doesn't speak a word of anything but Greek ... do you know the Greek for help?' He was making fun of her and he was enjoying himself, but she was terrified and furious with herself for letting him do this.

She swung, tense and stiff. 'You can't keep me here indefinitely.'

'I don't want to,' he said lazily. 'A few hours should exhaust your potential.'

Her cheeks burnt scarlet and her eyes flashed. Ben laughed. 'Oh, did that sting? Did you imagine I was abducting you to marry you?'

'I don't know what you think you're doing,' she lied.

'Come,' he mocked. 'Use your imagination.' He patted the bed. 'It's very comfortable. Try it.'

'Let me out, Ben.'

He settled himself as if he intended to stay for hours, his long body stretching on the bed and she felt her heart beating so hard it hurt.

'You don't even want me,' she said, and it hurt fiercely to say it aloud although she had thought it for hours.

'You'll do,' he shrugged.

'Why?' she asked, her voice breaking. 'You can't, Ben ... please!'

His eyes met hers, cold and contemptuous. 'Why do you think I came to Nice?'

'To get at Clea,' she said, because that had been clear for a long time.

He nodded. 'I had a plan and it was working very nicely until my damned father showed up.'

Joanne swallowed. 'What plan?'

'She destroyed my mother,' he said. 'She didn't do me much good, either. She had it coming to her.'

His eyes were jet black, icy, yet hectic, as though emotion were struggling like burning lava beneath the surface of that iciness.

If she could keep him talking she might get through to him somehow. She felt like someone dealing with a murderer, desperately trying to postpone any action.

'What were you going to do to her?' She sounded calm and that surprised her. It pleased her. Clea might not be able to act, but it appeared that she could, when the occasion demanded it.

'She thought I was going to back her film,' he said. 'She went around the party telling everyone. Once Sam Ransom knew, it would flash round the world. Clea would have done anything to get the money for that film.'

She flinched at that and his eyes swung to her sardonically. 'Oh, yes,' he said, 'anything. She's desperate. I got that from Lester. He wasn't even prepared to back the film alone. He wanted someone to share the risks. Clea has lost her box office appeal. She's finished if she doesn't make a good film quickly.'

Huskily she said, 'And when she'd told everyone, then, I suppose, you would have pulled out, leaving her looking very sick.'

Ben grinned. 'That would have been the curtain,' he said, nodding. 'But first I'd have got Clea so that she didn't know if she was coming or going.' He gave her a cold, confident smile. 'She was already promising me whatever I wanted in return for the cash.'

Her stomach heaved and she couldn't look at him. She bent her head and dew broke out on her temples. Would he have gone to bed with Clea? Was that what he meant? Oh, God, she thought, how far had he intended to go? The very idea of him with Clea made her sick.

'In the past she pulled the strings and the men danced,' he went on calmly. 'This time it was going to be different. I would pull the string and Clea would dance ... and it was working, too. She didn't feel sure of me: she showed it with every look she gave me. In time I'd have broken her the way she broke my mother.'

She had to know. In a rusty voice she asked, 'Had you made love to her?'

The dark eyes considered her, narrowed and mocking. 'Does it matter?'

Oh, yes, she thought, it matters. Aloud she said, 'Tell me.'

'That wasn't the idea,' he said, then, drily, 'On the contrary. She thought it was, of course. It was how she always operated. A quid pro quo basis ... she couldn't understand why I didn't grab what she was offering me, but she thought it would come.'

Joanne closed her eyes, limp with relief. He had not meant to take Clea at all. That had been his plan—to humiliate her by refusing her and then to dump the film too to complete the humiliation. And it would have hurt Clea. Oh, yes, it would have worked—if Jeb hadn't arrived on the scene.

There was a silence while she stared at the cabin floor and Ben lay there, watching her.

He moved slightly and her eyes flashed up, wide with anxiety. His mouth twisted coldly. 'Come here, Joanne.'

She shook her head. 'You're going to have to force

me, Ben, and if you do, I'll charge you with rape the minute I'm ashore again.'

He laughed, throwing back his head, the brown line of his throat powerful. 'Can you see yourself going into a police station and telling an incredulous policeman that Clea Thorpe's daughter wasn't willing?'

She flushed deeply, twisting her nails into her palms. 'I'd still tell them, whether they believed me or not.'

'Go ahead,' he shrugged indifferently, grinning with insolence. 'I really wouldn't give a damn. Either way I would get what I want.'

Joanne was bewildered, her eyes anxiously studying him.

'The press would eat it up,' he said, as if explaining something simple to a child. 'Can you see the headlines? Her career would really be finished.' His bland glance watched her with cold comprehension as she flinched. 'And do you really think my father could marry her after that?'

Then she realised just how trapped she was. If she brought a rape case against Ben the chances of Jeb marrying Clea were slim. There would be too much stacked against them.

She tried, though, her voice trembling. 'You would go to prison, though.'

'If they believed you,' he said softly. 'Nico would insist that you came aboard very willingly, that you came down here alone with me with a happy smile. I doubt if the charge would stick. And afterwards ... goodbye to Clea's career and her chance of marrying my father.'

'Oh, God!' she moaned, covering her face.

'There's no need for heroics,' he said. 'I won't hurt you.'

He would, she thought. Hurt her more than she could tolerate. He was inhuman, a monster of icy cruelty, and that her own mother had made him like this was ironic.

He moved off the bed, sighing, and she backed shaking her head. 'No, Ben!' He didn't even want to make love to her; he was merely doing it to hurt her mother. It was an act of cold revenge and he would destroy her if he did as he threatened. She would never be able to live with the memory.

He looked down into her white face in cold assessment. 'You were responsive enough last night,' he drawled. 'She's trained you well. You really turned me on, do you know that? That was when the idea came to me. I found myself wanting to go on and I thought, why not combine pleasure with revenge?'

Joanne shivered, staring at him. 'You can't do it to me,' she whispered. 'Could you live with yourself afterwards? Ben, think about it, for God's sake!'

He slid an arm around her waist, stooped and lifted her struggling into his arms, her legs kicking, her hands pushing at the wide brown shoulders. 'No!' she shrieked, suddenly frantic with fear and pain. 'No, Ben!'

He silenced her with his mouth and the hard, hot pressure deepened until she gave no more smothered cries, gasping for breath under his fierce kiss. Her hand went up to push his head away and stayed to touch his cheek, helplessly cradling his face, stroking his cool skin.

He lowered her to the bed and they stared at each other. She was breathing sharply, her eyes dazed.

His hand went to her hair and fiddled with the clasp, releasing it so that it tumbled down around her face. He moved his fingers through it, watching as it slid over his palm. 'You have sexy hair,' he said, and she found herself laughing, because it was so absurd, although the laughter died on her mouth at once.

Ben looked at her, his eyes ironic. 'I mean it,' he said. 'I've been wanting to touch it for days ... when you walk it flows over your shoulders like waves of black silk.'

She looked at him pleadingly. 'Ben, please!' He sounded almost gentle now and she thought she might get through to him, but he merely smiled, a cruel twist of his mouth, and his hands slid from her hair to her shoulders, spreading against them, fingers wide. He looked down at her body through lowered lids. 'Was Sam Ransom hoping to be your lover?' he asked casually.

'No!' she cried angrily.

'He was easier than that, was he? A few kisses and he was eating out of your hand. Of course, he doesn't fancy Clea. She's out of his age group. Sam likes them young.'

She struggled to get up and he pushed her down violently, his hands bruising. He framed her face between his palms and made her look at him. 'Am I the first? Tell me the truth, Joanne.'

Voicelessly she nodded, her lips dry.

He stared at her intently, then he bent his head and

began to kiss her, his mouth hungry, and she groaned, feeling the response rising inside her, knowing that she was not going to be able to refuse him.

Her arms went round his neck, she kissed him back, her eyes shut, and suddenly she did not care why he was making love to her, so long as he was, because her body was clamouring for him and she was drowning in a floodtide of desire which was too strong for her to fight.

Against her throat he whispered, 'In those things you look about sixteen, but it's a woman in my arms, Joanne...'

His fingers softly undid the buttons on the shirt while he kissed her ears and cheek and the lashes flickering on her skin. She groaned as she felt his hands touching her body, stroking her skin gently, sending shivers down her spine.

She tried to salvage her self-respect, racking her brains for a way of stopping him, but every touch, every movement of the long hard body beside her was sending her mind spinning off into outer space and she increasingly wanted to let him do whatever he wanted to do.

Huskily, she said, 'I thought wine was part of every good seduction scene.'

Ben lifted his head and the dark eyes smiled down at her. 'Why not? A little wine will certainly help you relax.' He moved and rang the bell on the wall, watching her through half-closed eyes. When the door opened and the Greek stood there, his eyes dancing with amusement as he looked towards Joanne and watched her drag her shirt together with shaking fingers, Ben said something in rapid Greek and the man nodded.

Joanne lay there, moistening her lips, waiting. The man went out and Ben went on watching her with a curiously wry face. When Nico came back with the wine Joanne got up. Ben came away from the wall, eyes intent.

'Shall I pour it?' she asked, walking towards the Greek, then swiftly picked up one of the wine glasses and threw it at Ben. He ducked and it splintered against the wall. Nico exclaimed something in Greek, staring, and while they were off guard Joanne ran for the door. She was through it and up the stairs, panting, before she heard Ben running after her, his bare feet stealthy on the wooden floor.

She dived down the ladder into the motor boat and started trying to work the engine, but nothing happened. Ben's face appeared over the side of the yacht. She glanced up desperately and he grinned at her mockingly.

'I've immobilised it,' he said softly. 'Tough luck, Joanne. A good try. Now come back here and we'll go on from where we were.'

She stood there, white-faced, staring at him. Then she threw off her shirt and unzipped her jeans. Ben's brows jerked together.

'Don't be a little fool!' he exclaimed, his tone changing.

She was over the side into the water before he had a foot on the ladder. She heard him shouting after her.

'You'll never make it, Joanne ... we're miles from shore!'

She was a good swimmer. She had been swimming since she was tiny and her strokes were strong and sure, but she knew as well as he did that her chances of reaching the beach were slim. Given the choice, though, she preferred to drown rather than let him do as he planned.

It took him some time to start the boat. She heard it coming after her and swam as hard as she could, her lungs bursting, her body weary. Ben circled her, the throttle closing, and came up beside her to drag her into the boat.

She dived down into the blue, blue water, holding her breath, and shot upward again some way away, her head exploding with the pain of holding her breath.

'You silly little bitch,' Ben yelled at her, returning in a circle once more. 'You'll drown!'

She ignored him, swimming on steadily. He leaned over the side and this time his hands fastened into her wet black hair. She winced at the pain he inflicted as he dragged her backwards and upwards. Kicking and fighting, she was hauled back into the boat.

'Let me go!' she panted, hitting out wildly.

He forced her down between his legs, holding her there, her head against his chest. For a moment they stayed quite still, both breathing heavily, then Ben pushed her head back, his fingers tangled in her hair, and stared into her eyes.

'You might have drowned,' he bit out.

'Preferable to what you had in mind,' she gasped breathlessly.

'Was it?' he asked flatly, staring at her without expression.

Joanne glared back, lips curling over her teeth. 'Yes,' she said defiantly.

Slowly he smoothed her wet hair down around her face, looking at her strangely. She was shivering as shock and exhaustion took hold of her and her teeth were chattering. He looked down at her almost naked body, the bra and briefs clinging wetly to her skin, moulding to her like a second skin.

'And if I hadn't bothered to come after you?' he asked drily.

A savage flare of pain took her by the throat and she said bitterly, 'I wish to God you hadn't!'

His face froze over. He turned and brought a blanket out from a locker, flung it round her, then started the engine again and headed for the shore. Joanne sat, wrapped in it, shuddering, watching the roofs and palm trees of Nice flashing closer and closer, and she wished he had left her to drown.

The sun had set by now and the beach was deserted in a warm twilight. Ben beached the boat and stepped out, lifting her out into his arms. 'I can walk,' she said stiffly.

He didn't answer. He moved up the cliff path carrying her, staring over her head. When they reached the garden she said huskily, 'Please, put me down ... I'm all right.'

He put her down as if she were a parcel he had carried. Without looking at him she shuffled into the changing rooms beside the swimming pool and found a towelling robe which they kept there. She slipped into it and tied the belt tight around her waist, then went out to give Ben back the blanket.

He had gone. Joanne looked towards the cliff path and saw only the evening shadows moving under the trees.

Slowly she turned and went into the house, leaving the blanket in the changing room. Milly looked up and stared at her. 'Swimming this late? It's much too cold.'

'Much too cold,' she agreed flatly, going upstairs. She was ice all the way through her body. By the skin of her teeth she had got out of Ben's trap, but she had left part of herself bleeding in it.

She would never be the same again; Ben had maimed her for life. She had come very close to letting him do as he liked with her and then she would have wanted to die. She wanted to die now. Shame, pain, humiliation, misery, tore at her like savage animals. She could not face Clea and Jeb tonight. She could not speak normally, pretend to be the same as she had been this morning. It had to show on her face. People must see what Ben had done to her.

She climbed into a warm nightdress and got into bed. Milly tapped on the door and came in, peering at her through the darkness. 'Headache?'

'Mmm,' she whispered.

'Poor Joanne,' Milly said, all sympathy. 'Going to sleep? That's right. It will have gone in the morning.'

It would not have gone, Joanne thought as Milly tiptoed out and closed the door. It would haunt her for the rest of her life. But she lay very still like a trapped animal pretending to be dead, and at last sleep caught her up and buried her in a brief oblivion.

In the morning she had recovered well enough to assume a calm mask which seemed to deceive Clea and Milly. She held it like a shield in front of her all day, smiling like a polite child when she had to, talking quietly.

Jeb spent the day with them and it was hard to look at him and not think of Ben. Every turn of his head, every intonation of his voice, reminded her. She tried not to look at him, but now and then she had to and it hurt.

He got her alone at some point and asked quietly, 'Is something wrong, Joanne?'

'Of course not,' she lied, smiling at him.

He watched her, frowning. 'Are you sure? You aren't upset because of Clea and myself, are you?'

She had to look at him then, to reassure him. 'No,' she said. 'I'm glad, very glad. You'll look after Clea.' Even if Clea's film career ended she would be safe now.

Jeb did not quite believe her. He was still concerned, but he was too intelligent to press the matter. She saw nothing of Ben that day, and as the days passed and she heard no word of him she knew he had gone away—to Paris, as he had told her, probably, and then to the States. She was relieved and yet she was aching. She hated and loved and she was torn between the two extremes. Sometimes she would have given anything just to see him; sometimes to see him would have been as bitter as hell.

They all flew back to the States two weeks later. Jeb was going to finance Clea's film, but first they were being married and going on a long honeymoon. Clea was radiant, childlike in her happiness, and looking at her

Joanne found it impossible to believe the things Ben had said about her. Could it be true that Clea had hinted at making him her lover? Had she promised that much? Joanne had no illusions about her mother's amorality. There had been too many men before him, but none of them had been on a strictly mercenary basis—Clea had always been in love, Joanne was sure of that. Her love affairs were passionate while they lasted, and maybe Ben had been wrong about that, maybe Clea had been attracted to him. After all, he was very like his father. That Clea might be marrying Jeb for his money might occur to anyone who did not know her, but Joanne did know her, and she was certain Clea's feelings were real and deep.

The press spread themselves on the subject of the wedding. Joanne read the speculation and gossip with angry eyes. Milly sighed, putting down Sam Ransom's paper. 'Did you read the story about Ben? They're hinting that he won't show up because he's sick with jealousy.'

Joanne had read it and it had hurt. But she said coolly enough, 'I doubt if he will come, but it will be because he's angry, not because he's jealous.'

Milly nodded. 'I don't see him turning up,' she agreed.

Neither did Jeb. He had sent his son an invitation to the wedding, but he told Joanne that he would put money on it that Ben did not come. 'It would be wisest if he did,' he said heavily. 'It would silence the gossip.'

Ben would not care about that. No doubt he hoped that the gossip would grow, would poison his father's marriage.

When Joanne finally told Clea and Jeb that she was going to England after the wedding, Clea began to cry and Jeb stared at Joanne with worried eyes. 'Why, Joanne?' he asked, and Clea cried harder, her hands over her face.

'I've never spent much time with my father,' Joanne explained. 'Now that Clea has you to rely on, I can go ... and I want to train for a job. I want to be independent.'

Clea lifted her head, her violet eyes tear-soaked. 'You're angry because of Jeb,' she wailed.

'Is that it?' Jeb asked, and Joanne assured him it was not, smiling at him.

'I'm glad, really glad about you and Clea.'

In the end she made them see that her mind was made up and Jeb talked Clea into accepting it, but Clea disliked change of any sort in her own household. Joanne had been part of her life for twenty years and Clea would miss her, just as she would miss Milly if she went, because Clea needed support; she was clinging ivy, she needed people to hold her up.

Joanne had chosen a very chic, sophisticated dress to wear at the wedding. The bodice fitted like a sheath, the material a fine smooth blue, darkening her eyes. It ran down over waist and hips tightly, flaring out at the knee in a layer of deep blue frills, ending at her calf. She wore her black hair in a chignon, a style she rarely wore, and she made up with care. When Milly saw her she eyed her with appreciation.

'I've never seen you look so pretty,' she said. 'We'll have to be careful you don't outshine Clea.'

They both laughed and it was a joke because Clea in

the cream silk she had chosen to wear looked so beautiful that at the wedding people stared and stared as if she were a vision which might vanish.

She was so happy she laughed all the time, and she looked at Jeb with adoration. Clea was going to be happy, Joanne could see that, and she was glad. She was glad, but she was going as far away as she could, because she had to get away from Clea, she had to forget if she could, although she did not believe it was possible. She had to escape from Clea's shadow and become herself, and most of all she had to try to put out of her mind what Clea had done to Ben and his mother, what Clea's involvement with Jeb had done to her through Ben. Clea must never know it, but she had ruined Joanne's life as well as Ben's.

Jeb she was fond of, she admired and liked him. He had learnt a poker face. He was adept at concealing his emotions. His passion for Clea apart, she suspected, he was a hard businessman, determined to get his own way, as arrogant and self-assertive as his son, but more human, a man of humour even if it was irony, a man with a vein of warmth running through the cold granite of his nature. Ben was all granite. There was no human weakness in him.

At the reception after the wedding, Joanne hovered in the background well out of sight, watching the guests greeting Clea and Jeb, admiring her mother's radiant beauty with rueful eyes.

She saw Ben suddenly and the shock rocked her where she stood. She went white and for a moment she was unguarded, her eyes agonised. Jeb happened to be looking at her and his eyes narrowed in his hard face.

Then he looked round and he saw Ben, too, and glanced back quickly at Joanne, but she was already pulling a mask over her face, assuming a calm she did not feel.

Ben walked towards them with a lovely blonde girl hanging on his arm. She was a typical model, long-legged, swaying, her mouth wearing a plastic smile.

Joanne walked away and pretended to get herself a glass of champagne. From a distance she saw Ben lightly brush Clea's flushed cheek, saw him shake hands with his father, a cool smile on his face. He looked at ease and unconcerned and the buzzing whispers did not seem to reach him.

Photograpers snapped around them, flashbulbs exploding like lightning, and Ben's face remained smilingly cool.

Ben's pride had brought him here today, Joanne guessed now. He would not allow anyone to believe that Clea had hurt him, that he was jealous or angry. He had come to make a public declaration of acceptance to dispel the scandal which had gathered around the marriage.

Sam Ransom made his way through the crowd towards Joanne, his eyes curious. She smiled at him as he joined her and he said, 'Who would have expected that? Did you know he was coming?'

'Of course,' she lied, smiling sweetly. 'Why not? He brought them back together, didn't he?'

'He did?' Sam stared at her incredulously. 'Are you saying that Ben engineered it all? That he came to smooth Jeb's way for him?'

Joanne didn't answer, just smiled and smiled, and

Sam was not sure what to believe. Famous people did the craziest things and Sam did not find it easy to believe that someone of his own age, like Ben Norris, would fall for Clea Thorpe, despite her fame. Sam never had. She was outside his age group and Sam, as Ben had said, liked his women younger than himself.

Ben had certainly vanished once Jeb appeared on the scene, so Sam shrugged and filed the interpretation away for future reference. Next day his column was headed JEB'S SON PLAYS CUPID, and the other reporters read it and cursed because it was exclusive and their editors wanted to know why he had it and they didn't.

Ben stayed for an hour. Joanne kept well away from him, watching him from a safe distance whenever his head was turned away from her. He flirted with the blonde lightly, a glass in his hand, a charming smile on that hard mouth. Joanne allowed Sam to stay glued to her side. She smiled at him and joked with him, and Sam's eyes were curious and wry as he talked to her. He had not forgotten her behaviour the night he kissed her in the garden, but Joanne was hiding any emotion from him now and he was not certain what was in her mind.

Ben moved to the door after saying goodbye to Clea and Jeb and Joanne turned to watch him for the last time. She wondered if she would ever see him again, and hoped she wouldn't, because the pain she was feeling now was enough to last a lifetime.

He turned at the door and his eyes moved across the room; she knew he was looking for her, that he had known where she was all the time he was in the room, although they had never once looked at each other.

Across the chattering, crowded room their eyes met as if across a chasm. Joanne drank in the arrogant tilt of his black head, the hard bones of the face, the cool dark eyes set under those thin, ironic brows. Her face was distant, withdrawn to a safe place where he could not reach her. She stood there, her glass in her hand, a slender, graceful girl in a chic blue dress, her black hair shining under the lights, and her eyes gave nothing away.

Ben turned away and went out. The noise, the light, seemed to fade and she was alone in blackness for a moment. Then her eyes blinked once and she lifted her glass to her lips and drank thirstily, rapidly, letting the race of the champagne in her blood lift her spirits from the misery in which they were sunk.

When Clea and Jeb had flown off on their honeymoon she said goodbye to Milly with real regret and sadness, packed and flew to England, feeling as if she left behind her old life as the plane lifted up into the cloudless blue sky.

CHAPTER FIVE

HER father was oddly unsurprised to see her. She had cabled her arrival in advance, of course, but when she was shown into his office at the hotel, he merely smiled and came to kiss her, asking her no questions. Only later did she realise that he took her arrival so soon after Clea's second marriage to mean that Jeb had not wanted her around. She did not disillusion him since for the moment she was unwilling to discuss the subject with anyone. Her best hope for recovery from the wounds inflicted by Ben was, she had decided, total silence, in the hope that her feelings towards him would be swallowed in the oblivion of forgetfulness.

'So you're planning a secretarial career?' her father asked her with an approving smile. He had aged far more than either Clea or Jeb, Joanne realised, surveying him with a measuring eye. His hair was thinning and receding from his placid temples, his eyes were heavily lined, his figure heavy and stooping.

They might have been total strangers as they sat drinking coffee together in the quiet backwater of the office, among the grey steel filing cabinets and the wide leather-topped desk. They spoke to each other courteously, carefully.

'I need a job,' she said. 'That seems the best. I have no talents or leaning in any other direction.'

'Why not start here in the hotel?' he asked, without pressing her. 'We run a good secretarial agency for our guests. It's small but very efficient. You could do a secretarial course part-time while working here to get experience.'

It was a splendid idea and she was delighted. He looked pleased and amused when she broke into smiles, her eyes shining. 'Could I really?' She had not really looked forward to going back to school full-time. Being at work some of the time would make the learning part of it easier. She could feel she was an adult, useful, someone who had a proper job to do.

Also, she thought, looking at her father, she might at last get to know him on his own ground. She had always been an outsider, a visitor, someone who must be treated with kid gloves. Now she would be on the inside for a change, getting to know how he and Angela really lived, being part of their daily lives.

'I'd love it,' she said, quite unnecessarily, since her pleasure had been so plain to see, and her father laughed.

'Wait until you've worked here before you say that,' he urged with a complacent look. He loved hotel living. He loved everything about his work. He had no fear that Joanne would be bored or restless. She saw that, and she in turn was amused by him.

A faint anxiety clouded her eyes. 'You will give me a real job?' she asked him pleadingly. She had worked for Clea for so long without ever feeling she was truly part of that life. 'I want to be just another secretary.'

John Ross's eyes twinkled. 'You will,' he assured her. 'Wait until you meet Erma.'

She raised enquiring brows.

'Come and meet her now,' he said, his mouth twitching.

The secretarial agency was situated on the ground floor of the hotel, shut away behind glazed doors which were, she realised as they opened, quite soundproof. As she entered the long, rectangular room the rattle of typewriters hit her ears like gunfire. Girls sat at desks in two rows between which ran an alley which led to a glass box. Inside it, like a witch in a fairy tale, sat a woman of middle years. Her skin was oily and sallow, her black hair twisted in a thick rope which was laid neatly across the crown of her head, a hairstyle Joanne had never seen before. Her dark eyes were melancholic and, like a policeman's, saw everything in all directions, as was proved when the girls broke into a buzz of soft comment as John Ross and Joanne entered. The woman shot out of the box, clapping her hands together in a peremptory manner. 'Silence! No talking!'

'Fudge,' Joanne heard someone somewhere whisper. Her lips broke into a smothered smile and she half turned her head to meet impudent hazel eyes which scrutinised her curiously.

Joanne grinned and got an answering grin, a fleeting wink, then the girl looked back at her work, her fingers flying over the keys.

'Erma,' her father said, taking her arm and swinging her towards the other woman, 'this is Joanne, my daughter. Can you find a desk for her? Some easy work? She's going to take a secretarial course, but until she can do shorthand and typing I want you to make use of her, teach her office work.'

Joanne met the dark eyes a little warily. The woman seemed to be a martinet and she wanted no trouble. But Erma was smiling, a peculiarly sweet, warm smile. 'Joanne, I'm pleased to meet you.' She had an accent which Joanne could not place. Foreign, certainly, and that hairstyle, the whole look of her suggested an Eastern European origin. Poland ... Hungary ... somewhere behind the Iron Curtain.

Erma looked around the room. 'A desk,' she said. 'Let me see ...' She pointed to one which was empty. 'You can have that one. I shall put you next to someone who can be helpful.'

Joanne looked hopefully towards the girl with hazel eyes, but Erma called, 'Sharon!' A thin, brisk girl looked up and came towards them, her face politely expressionless. 'Look after Joanne,' said Erma. 'Give her some envelopes to type.' She smiled at Joanne. 'Sharon will show you how to centre them correctly, then you can work as slowly as you need to ... there is no hurry. If you make a mistake, throw the envelope away and start again. Accuracy is more important than speed.'

John Ross nodded, smiled and left. As soon as the door had closed behind him Joanne became aware of a change in the atmosphere. Erma seemed to relax. The girls seemed to become noisier, their silence giving way to muted chatter. Erma went back to her glass box and Sharon took Joanne to her desk and began demonstrating how to type an envelope.

'I can't type,' Joanne pointed out.

'It doesn't matter,' Sharon shrugged. 'Use one finger if you have to ... just plod away. It's a boring job and we all hate it.'

Joanne looked at her, and Sharon grinned. 'I meant typing envelopes,' she said. 'Not working here.'

'It can be fun working here,' said a light voice. Joanne turned and found herself facing the hazel-eyed girl.

'Hi! I'm Annie.'

Looking back five years later, Joanne remembered that moment very clearly. She could see the office, the girls at their desks, the sun streaming in through the windows, and she could hear the voice saying, 'Hi! I'm Annie.'

Meeting Annie that day had, although at the time she had been unaware of it, formed an indissoluble link.

Some friendships are like that. They are landmarks in life. Most people one meets are just ships passing in the night, casual, forgettable, forgotten. Once in a while one meets someone who makes an instant visual impact and continues to do so year after year. Annie West was a landmark in Joanne's life.

Although it had been Sharon who was put in charge of her, it was Annie to whom she turned for help and advice from the start. Sharon had been mortally offended. An efficient, self-important girl, she knew that she was far more capable than Annie and she resented the fact that Joanne preferred to ask Annie's advice, to giggle and chatter to her, rather than to follow Sharon's example and work away like a white mouse on a wheel.

Annie was still attending secretarial school. Joanne joined her there and found she enjoyed the technical skills she was acquiring. She learnt to type with a blind keyboard, the letters covered so that she could not see them and had to learn to touch-type. She practised whenever she could and her speed soon began to mount. She practised her shorthand, too, taking down bits of the news or five minutes of a short story on the radio. Annie was too frivolous to do either. 'What are you doing?' she would demand. 'Oh, gawd, put your halo away and switch to Radio One!'

By then they were sharing a flat. Joanne had had the idea. Her father wanted her to live at the hotel, but she had had enough of being on tap night and day with Clea. She wanted independence, freedom, her own scene . . . she wanted a place of her own.

'I can't let you live alone in London,' her father said anxiously. He was pleased that she had decided to stay with him rather than return to her mother. By now she had explained to him that Jeb had not flung her out of the nest to find her own path. Jeb had wanted her to stay on—it had been Joanne's decision to leave. 'I wanted to get to know my other family,' she had said, and her father had looked gratified. But he wanted her to live in the hotel, not to go off alone to live in a flat. He had nightmares about homicidal maniacs breaking into the flat and murdering her in her bed. He did not say so, but worse visions visited his mind.

Joanne saw his point, even the thoughts he did not mention. She listened as he outlined the various horrors which could befall her alone in London, and her brain presented a solution.

'Share a flat?' Annie had grinned, then groaned. 'I'd love to, but they cost the earth and my salary won't stretch to it.' She lived with her parents and three younger brothers in Watford, travelling in and out of the capital, lemming-like, cramped in with all the other lemmings in a tube, suffocated and irritable. Her eyes sparkled at the thought of living in London and being free to enjoy city life without parental restraints.

Joanne shyly, hesitantly, explained that she was taking a year's lease of a flat and would only ask Annie to pay a low rent. 'I can only take a flat if someone shares it with me,' she said. It was embarrassing to make the offer, but Annie was a realist. She knew that Joanne had money of her own; her background made that clear. Annie saw no reason why she should make Joanne's money a barrier. Money to her meant something to spend. She had a hedonistic attitude to life. Today was what mattered—forget tomorrow.

The flat was in Islington, the ground floor of a tall terraced house split into flats. They each had a room of their own, a shared kitchen and bathroom, a communal sitting-room. 'Heaven!' Annie had laughed their first day, whirling around the rooms like a dervish. 'Oh, what fun we'll have!'

It had been fun. Joanne found her first taste of freedom heady. She and Annie crammed a lot into their spare hours. London was a big city, but they got to know a lot of it. They got buses and tubes from one end of it to the other. They visited parks, shops, cinemas. They made friends, particularly Annie. She was a lively, energetic girl who attracted people like a magnet. Joanne had a quieter nature, but she was determined to shake off the repression which Clea had unwittingly led her to impose on her own character. 'Come out of your shell,' Annie told her, and Joanne did.

She learnt to talk to people, she altered her hairstyle and her way of dressing, she threw herself into enjoyment wholeheartedly.

At the hotel she soon found herself as competent as the other girls. Annie could not be bothered to work hard at her job, but Joanne quite enjoyed having the skills needed for a good secretary, and she soon rose in the office by her own efforts. Erma appeared to be delighted. She had been afraid Joanne would be playing at work and when she saw she was not, she encouraged her eagerly. They worked in the hotel pool unless a guest needed secretarial assistance, when they went off to work as required, taking down letters or sitting in on business conferences. The hotel specialised in these.

They had a conference centre, highly equipped, with all the modern machinery demanded for such occasions. The conference hall was spacious and comfortable. They got visitors from other countries and had translation cubicles, headphones and all the other paraphernalia required.

It was a varied, interesting life. Joanne got up each morning eager for work, while Annie had to be shaken out of bed. Yawning, she would trail around, groaning. Erma sighed over her. But Annie was popular with guests who did not demand too high a standard of secretarial work. They liked her too much to complain. Erma was wry about that. 'One day,' she would say threateningly. 'One day, Annie ... goodbye ... unless you work harder.'

Annie did not care. She was enjoying herself, although mostly out of office hours. They had parties in the flat, went to parties elsewhere. They each met men, gradually got steady boy-friends. Joanne learnt soon enough to suppress her relationship to Clea. Her surname was Ross, of course, which meant that unless she brought it up few people ever connected her with her mother. Men who found out behaved as though she had done them some injury. They seemed to believe she cheated by being herself while being Clea Thorpe's daughter. Joanne had learnt to maximise her own looks, but she could not turn herself into a raving beauty without a magic spell, and those were far beyond her.

In five years she had three steady boy-friends ... Annie called them 'Joanne's little mistakes.' With each one she went through the same pattern. She met them, liked them, drifted into a close relationship and got after a time to the point of permanency. Marriage would be mentioned: the same thing happened every time. Joanne always knew when that point was approaching, yet when it arrived she was always stricken with fear and panic.

She could not explain it even to herself. After the breakup of each affair she was utterly miserable. She felt guilty and alarmed. 'Why worry?' Annie would ask lightly. 'Marriage is for the birds.' She flitted like a butterfly from flower to flower, enjoying herself, and she had no intention of settling down. She could not see why Joanne worried so much about the men she discarded. 'They'll get over you,' she said, and she was right, of course. They did. But Joanne found it depressing that they should. Did no relationship mean anything? Was life always so shifting and impermanent?

When Annie informed her suddenly, after five years, that she was getting married, Joanne was shaken. Annie laughed, shaking her head. 'He's a bulldog,' she said, referring to Roger, the man she was going to marry. 'He won't let go.' She had known him for a year, but there had been others in that time and Joanne was puzzled and worried. Was Annie making a fatal mistake?

'But are you sure?'

'I'm ready to marry,' Annie assured her. 'I knew I was when I started looking in prams.' She pretended to shudder. 'The beginning of the end!'

Joanne laughed. 'You want babies?'

'No,' said Annie. 'But I'm going to need them. When you start looking in prams and cooing, you've had it.' A dreamy expression came into her eyes. 'I might even learn to knit. Yellow bootees ... don't you love yellow bootees? Have you ever looked at the sole of a baby's foot? It's like a map of the world ... all lines and wrinkles.' Her eyes glowed. 'Roger's babies will have enormous noses, like the Duke of Wellington ... old Hooky, they used to call him ... I think I'll call Roger that. Can you imagine a baby with his nose? Poor little mite!'

The wedding was chaotic and delightful. Everyone had a wonderful time, especially Annie. She raced around in her white dress and floating veil, glowing with happiness. Roger just stood there, solid and smiling, his broad figure like a rock in the whirlpool Annie set up around him, but Joanne felt the happiness radiating out of him whenever she went near him.

Annie left the office and went off to the Midlands with Roger to live and work. Joanne had moved up the office by now to become the chief secretary under Erma. Annie's going left her alone in the flat which she now had on a ten-year lease. It seemed big and empty without Annie. She felt life fold in on her, her days a blank. She had established a habit from the start of spending one evening a week with her father and Angela. Patricia and David were not on her wavelength, but she felt impelled to make the effort to get to know them. Long before Annie's marriage, both of them had married and got homes of their own. Patricia had a baby, a squat, complacent infant with flushed cheeks and bottle green eyes who behaved perfectly day and night, according to Patricia. David preferred life without nappies and gripewater, he said. He put off the problems of a family, electing instead to enjoy a comfortable existence in his nice, elegant little house with his nice, elegant wife.

Deirdre was capable and kind-hearted, but Joanne found her as dull as she did David. However, when they invited her to dinner parties she often went, to please her father, who liked to feel that she was now part of his family. Joanne suspected he had a slight guilt complex about having left her with Clea. He thought she had had a bad childhood and he blamed himself.

Although Annie had gone, she had left an indelible mark upon Joanne. The quiet, withdrawn girl who had come to England in flight from the pain Ben had inflicted had become a woman of twenty-six with a cool manner, a good dress sense and a calm self-confidence which could make quite an impression when she chose.

It was at one of David's dinner parties that she met Ralph Brent. He was a chartered accountant with an office in Kensington. Tall, sober, good-looking, he was clearly attracted to Joanne on sight, and she found him a good companion. Ralph dated her, taking her carefully to the sort of place he felt one should be seen at: he had a taste for discreetly luxurious decor and good food, and a passion for being fashionable.

He met her father and they liked each other at once. Angela was enthusiastic about him. 'Now, don't lose this one,' she urged, and Joanne felt her teeth grit irritably, but she laughed, pretending to be amused. Angela was inclined to state the obvious, unaware of the effect this could have on those around her.

If anything could have put her off Ralph it would have been the seal of approval he received from her family. David beamed on them, feeling like the onlie begetter of their relationship ... 'A good chap,' he told Joanne. And she heard the silent echo of Angela's words: don't lose him. David did not say so; he knew better. But he thought it and his eyes said it. Joanne was on the shelf—she knew that was how her father's family saw her. Their pitying, irritated eyes told her as much. There was no reason for it, they told each other. Joanne was attractive, intelligent, assured. She dressed beautifully now. She knew how to listen as well as how to talk. Her unmarried state puzzled them. They could only decide it was her fault. Somehow she frightened off the men who came too near.

Angela took it on herself to explain this to Joanne. 'You're too self-contained, my dear. You must try to be more approachable.'

Joanne could have screamed. Instead she said, 'I'll remember. Thank you, Angela.' The polite terms on which they met were maintained only by scrupulous care on Joanne's part. She knew that if she ever let her hair down she would fling home-truths at Angela like balls at a coconut shy. Angela would never forgive her and the whole careful edifice she had erected over the past five years would crash down around her ears. So she smiled and held her tongue, although it galled her to pretend to be grateful for advice which maddened her.

During the past five years she had seen her mother only three times. Clea preferred the sunnier climes of the world and rarely visited England. Joanne had received invitations to Nice and the States, but she had pleaded various excuses. When Clea and Jeb came over to see her she was very careful to erase from their minds any suspicions of sulking or bitterness in her attitude. Jeb had proved himself more than capable of managing Clea. Joanne saw, with amusement, that her mother relied upon him now for everything. Milly said wryly to her, 'She should have married him years ago. It works, Joanne—it really works.' Milly still performed her necessary functions as Clea's secretary. Jeb had kept his word. Clea had lost nothing—except her daughter. And Joanne knew that Clea did not miss her. Although she was affectionate when they met, Clea was vague, as she always had been, her life so full that Joanne was barely missed.

It was Milly who wrote to Joanne. Once a week the blue envelopes arrived bearing the news Milly considered she should know. Ben's name was never mentioned, and Joanne got the impression they never saw or heard from him.

The only time Ben was mentioned was when Jeb gave up his business to become part of Clea's travelling circus. Ben took over control of the firm, Milly said. The sight of his name gave Joanne a shock which made her skin go cold.

Jeb was soon the ringmaster of the circus. He took control of Clea's business affairs and managed both them and her with supreme competence.

The last time they had visited England Joanne saw with a shock that her mother was beginning to age. The gloss of beauty was wearing down, as if time wiped a sponge over Clea's face and left a blurred image where once the clear-cut mask had drawn the eyes. Her skin was slackening, her throat growing lined, her mouth losing that radiant curve, her eyes becoming less brilliant.

It could have been a tragedy, but Jeb saw to it that it was not. Under his guidance she began to take a different sort of role. Her film career changed slowly, imperceptibly. She had relied on her looks; now she began to act, and the years of being around film studios watching other actresses paid off. Clea astonished the film world by actually being able to act. Those who had sneered, calling her 'The Face', were confounded. Milly told Joanne of evenings when Jeb sat with Clea teaching her how to project emotions, to reproduce the feelings of the part she would play. Clea, parrot-like, learnt the words and Jeb told her what they meant. She had always played herself—it was an easy part. Now she had to get herself under the skin of others and, having been a beauty all her life, she did not find that easy. Jeb showed her how to do it and she learnt fast.

When Milly wrote to say that they would be coming to England again, Joanne found herself curious about what she would see. From Milly's letters it had become clear that Clea had altered considerably under Jeb's influence, just as Joanne had altered under Annie's. People did that to each other; they came casually into contact and were somehow changed. It was a chemical reaction one could never foresee.

It had never occurred to Joanne that Ralph had had some sort of influence on her until Milly stared at her, her sandy hair now grey, and said, 'You've changed. Ralph, I suppose.'

There was disparagement in her tone and Joanne bridled. 'Don't you like him?'

'No,' Milly said cheerfully. 'Not particularly. He's dull, isn't he?'

Joanne was startled and irritated. 'Certainly not!'

'No? Well, you know him better than I do ... but at first sight, I'd call him dull.' Milly was indifferent. She reverted to the subject which still engrossed all her attention. 'How do you think Clea is looking?'

'Older,' Joanne said, sobering.

Milly sighed. 'Yes.' She did not dispute it. 'She's over fifty.'

'It shows.' Joanne did not mean to be cruel, but it was the truth. Five years ago Clea had looked ten years younger than her age. Now that her age was beginning to show she looked almost pathetic to her daughter. Joanne had never felt sorry for Clea before, and it was a painful experience.

'Her last film got better reviews than anything she's ever done before.' Milly was almost aggressive.

'I know. I read them.'

'Jeb has been marvellous for her.' Milly was trying to convince her and Joanne needed no convincing.

'He's a wonderful man. A pity they didn't get together sooner.'

Milly stared at her. 'Why don't you come back, Joanne? She would be so pleased.'

Joanne smiled, wry but not bitter. 'She hardly knows I'm not there. Come on, Milly, admit it. Clea doesn't need me.'

Milly did. She sighed. 'I miss you. While Clea is at the studio I miss you all the time. There's nobody to talk to ... the place is like a morgue. Jeb goes along with Clea and I feel as if I'm on a desert island.'

Joanne was sorry for her. 'Milly, I'm sorry. I've got my own life here in London, though. There's Ralph . . .'

'Ralph!' Milly snorted. She looked at Joanne, shaking her head. 'You're half alive. What's happened to you? Is this what you want out of life?'

It was a question which pricked the bubble of Joanne's complacence. She had gradually grown accustomed to her efficient, organised way of life. It was a shell into which she had slipped unaware. Now she became aware of it and it worried her.

'Your father may like this sort of life, but it isn't for you,' Milly added, and Joanne was silenced.

Then she remembered the pain which she had carried around for months after she last saw Ben and she knew why she lived as she did—it was safer and easier. Ralph offered her security, kindness, calm affection. She could give him back that affection. She liked him; she admired him. Her mouth twisted. He could not hurt her —and that was his chief quality.

Her life might not be very exciting, but at least it did not hurt. She had sworn to herself that she would never again become exposed to the sort of pain she had felt over Ben. She had grown a hard skin around her heart, and she intended to keep it.

'Ralph suits me,' she said firmly.

Milly made a face. 'Then you've changed out of all recognition,' she said, and it was true. Joanne had changed. She had meant to, it had been a deliberate, thought-out decision.

Jeb shared Milly's views. He got Joanne alone to tell her so, and he was just as blunt. 'Ralph is a bore,' he said.

'He suits me,' she told him, as she had told Milly, and like Milly he made a face.

'I don't believe it.'

'What's wrong with Ralph?' she chose to be flippant. 'He washes behind his ears and he changes his shirt twice a day.'

'That's what's wrong with him.' Jeb could be flippant too, but there was serious thought behind his wry smile. 'Joanne, you're just playing safe.' His insight startled her and she looked stricken. He pressed his advantage. 'Life's a gamble. You have to take a risk. You don't care for Ralph, Joanne—admit it.'

Her mouth set stubbornly. 'Ralph is what I want.'

'No,' said Jeb. 'Ralph is what you're settling for ... we both know what you want.'

She went scarlet and her eyes were furious. Without a word she turned and left him, and Jeb made a sound of irritation with himself.

Clea's arrival on the scene like a comet, trailing clouds of glory, had unsettled Ralph. He had, of course, known about Joanne's famous mother. She had felt safe in telling him about Clea because Ralph was so cool-headed, but it was one thing to know about the relationship, it was another to see Joanne beside Clea, make the obvious comparison, and Ralph found it baffling.

'You're nothing like her,' he said, and for a moment Joanne had looked furious, then she heard the note of satisfaction in his voice and her eyes froze on his face.

'She's rather shallow,' Ralph added. Clea had put herself out to be nice to him. She did not share Jeb and Milly's view of him. He was a good-looking man, well-dressed, courteous and attentive, and that was good enough for Clea. It surprised Joanne that Ralph should be critical, considering the charm with which Clea had flattered him when they met.

Ralph was very serious-minded, however. Clea, beautiful though she still was, had not impressed him with her intelligence. 'That secretary of hers does all the work,' said Ralph. He had noted that. He liked women to be capable. He expected them to organise themselves. Joanne did, and that was one of her attractions for him.

After they were married he expected her to go on working. He wanted a family, he said, but in time, not immediately. They would plan their life soberly. Ralph knew exactly the sort of house he wanted, exactly how it must be furnished. 'There's no rush,' he said, and what he meant was that he was in no hurry to change his life-style. He liked it the way it was, calm, organised, tidy. Joanne would fit in nicely. They would have a pleasant life together. A child would blow a hole in Ralph's scheme of things.

'I always planned to marry when I was thirty-five,' he had told her, with a smile meant to convey ironic amusement. 'But there you are . . .' He felt that in altering his plan for Joanne he had done enough. She must do the rest. If they married, they would maintain the gracious standards he wanted and Joanne would see to it that she did not make waves.

Jeb's open disapproval of him puzzled him. He admired Jeb. Ralph would always admire success and Jeb had been very successful. 'He must be a millionaire ten times over,' Ralph commented.

'Easily,' Joanne admitted. She was indifferent. It

made no impact on her, all that money.

Ralph eyed her disapprovingly. 'Money matters,' he said.

'It's what makes the world go round,' she agreed, half flippantly.

'It certainly does.' Ralph did not find money amusing. It was a serious subject.

She smiled at him, admitting to herself that sometimes he bored and irritated her. Nobody is perfect, though, she thought. Ralph is kind, Ralph is good-tempered, Ralph is thoughtful. She recited his good qualities often. It helped to fix them in her mind.

When he kissed her she responded exactly as he wished her to, knowing by now exactly the order of response he needed. She was warm without being passionate, submissive without being clinging.

After all, nobody could live in a vacuum. One had to have people, an inhabited world. Life could not be a desert island. When she chose to leave Clea and come to England she had, in fact, chosen to live as her father lived, to make the same sort of life he had made for himself. Ralph, she admitted ruefully, was her male equivalent of Angela. He fitted in with the quiet, painless world she wanted to have around her.

While Clea and Jeb were staying in London, Ralph decided it was the proper time for them to become formally engaged. They had had an understanding for some time, but Ralph liked to do things in the right way. He invited Clea, Jeb, John Ross and Angela to dinner. 'What, all of them?' Joanne asked incredulous. During their visits to London Clea and Jeb had avoided meeting Joanne's father and stepmother, and although

John Ross had no apparent grudge against his former wife Joanne thought it on the whole sensible of them to stay apart. Ralph, however, smiled complacently.

'Of course. They're civilised, my dear. It's years since your parents were divorced. Why, I imagine they're strangers to each other—perfect strangers.'

Joanne eyed him. 'I hope you're right.'

Ralph was amused. Of course he was right. Wasn't he always? 'I realise that you see them in a different light,' he said comfortingly. 'But as a neutral observer I think I see them pretty clearly.'

Her father and Angela could be trusted to behave like angels, Joanne thought, but Clea? Ralph did not know Clea.

'Do you think she'll make any trouble?' she asked Milly on the phone, her voice slightly panic-stricken.

Milly was dubious. 'Since she married Jeb her fits of mischief have stopped.' But although she said that, she sounded uncertain.

'I don't trust her!' Joanne was wailing and she knew it. Where men were concerned Clea was unpredictable. God knows what she would do face to face with her ex-husband.

'Jeb will keep a tight rein on her.' Milly had come to rely on him, she trusted him, but so far Jeb had not had any really sticky situation to deal with, and this, heaven alone knew, was as sticky a situation as he was likely to meet. Joanne wished she had Milly's confidence.

The dinner party was the occasion on which Ralph intended to bestow his engagement ring on her publicly. He would, she sensed, make speeches: Ralph had been trained in public speaking. 'Is anyone?' she asked him, dumbfounded. 'What do you do? Have mock dinners and toastmasters?' And Ralph had said, 'Don't be frivolous, darling. It doesn't suit you.' But then what did? Joanne looked at herself in the mirror with misgivings and wondered if anything suited her. She was beginning to feel more and more lost. She had come to England to find herself after years in Clea's shadow and although the five years with Annie had given her plenty of fun and freedom, she had come out of it with no clear idea of who she was, after all. Annie had got a husband and the prospect of babies in yellow bootees. Joanne had ended up with an assured manner, good dress sense, a well-paid career and Ralph, and all that added up to was a big question mark.

If she had asked everyone exactly what sort of person she was, she would have got a wide variety of different answers. 'I'm a chameleon,' she thought. She looked at herself again and felt as though she were looking at a stranger.

Then she went off to work, her teeth gritted. She would make her marriage to Ralph work. She would forge some sort of life for herself. Ralph would never set the world on fire, but she didn't want a fireraiser, she wanted a good husband, a man she could trust, and Ralph was that, all right ... he was dependable, he was predictable, he was concrete from his well-polished shoes to his well-brushed hair.

Joanne ran the office now under Erma. They had become friends in five years. She knew about Erma's early life in pre-war Poland. She knew about the misery of her wartime experience there, about her marriage to a British soldier and arrival, speaking only seven words of English, in a London so big and noisy that Erma felt sick for days. She knew about her little house, her pots of geraniums, her two cats and one son, her three grandchildren and their passion for bubble-grum.

'Bubblegrum?' she had enquired, keeping her face straight.

Erma had gazed at her placidly. 'It blows big bubbles.'

And Joanne had laughed. 'I know the stuff you mean.' She liked Erma. They worked well together. Since Annie left, Erma was the closest friend she had.

Today Erma looked distraught. 'What's wrong?' Joanne asked.

'In the Napoleon Suite,' Erma said breathlessly, 'there is a man ...'

Joanne's eyes rounded. Erma had a telegraphic style of talking which could make her giggle. 'What did he do? Molest you?'

Erma laughed, her mouth wide, her eyes sparkling, then, sobering, said, 'He is impossible! Three girls have I sent him. Three girls he has sent back, the last one cried for half an hour. He shouts and he sends rude letters.'

'Who to?'

'To me, who to?' Erma said indignantly. She waved a small sheaf of papers. 'Such words, incompetent, stupid ... what does he want?'

'A punch on the nose, by the sound of it,' said Joanne, militant. 'I'll sort him out.'

It was what Erma wanted. Her English deserted her faced by masculine aggression. She beamed on Joanne. 'Please!'

Joanne knocked on the door of the Napoleon Suite, her face masked in icy efficiency. The suites were used by the top men of the huge companies who used the hotel for conferences. They were luxuriously furnished, very masculine in decor, with leather armchairs and studded nails in the upholstery of square-built chairs. The hotel's interior decorator used psychology in his choice of colours, assertive, bold and yet solid. Maybe it's the setting, she thought, waiting for the door to open, which turns an ordinary managing director into Attila the Hun. All that leather and honed wood gives them ideas of conquest. Secretaries become slaves at their chariot wheels.

The door was flung open and a man stood there, naked to the waist, his face and hair damp, a towel in his hand. He stared at her and she stared back, the colour draining from her face, her body clenched against the stab of a shock which was almost intolerable.

'What the hell are you doing here?' Ben asked.

CHAPTER SIX

JOANNE pulled herself together with an effort. 'I might ask the same of you!' she retorted, and she needed all her courage to answer him at all because she knew perfectly well that she was suffering from all the symptoms of acute physical shock, her skin cold, her heart thudding, her breathing fast.

He had altered, she saw, as she looked at him through eyes which saw darkly at first and only began to clear slowly. He had always resembled his father very closely. The resemblance was now quite striking. Even the black hair was beginning to show a few fine threads of silver. But Ben's face had a hard arrogance which lacked Jeb's humour and vein of humanity. The dark eyes studied her icily, the strong features remained unlit with any warmth or courtesy. My God! she thought. He isn't human.

'I'm waiting,' he said through his teeth. 'What do you want? How did you know I was here?'

She flushed and anger made her fluent. 'I didn't. I work here—I'm employed by the Hotel Secretarial Agency. You asked for a secretary; I'm it.'

His mouth twisted. 'You? A secretary?'

'A good one,' she threw back, her chin lifting in defiance.

'Really?' The tone was sardonic.

'Really,' she snapped, barely able to control a desire to slap his handsome face.

A floor maid passed along the corridor, eyeing them curiously, and Ben stepped back, waving Joanne into his suite. Closing the door, he lifted his towel as though he had forgotten until now that he held it and slowly dried his face. She watched, mouth dry. His bare shoulders and chest had that physical magnificence she remembered and it infuriated her. He was bronzed and fit, his skin wearing a smooth uniform tan which could only have been acquired by long hours of exposure to the sun. The muscles in arms and shoulders rippled as he tossed the towel over a chair. He thrust back his dark hair with one hand and picked up a clean shirt, shouldering into it, his eyes on her face.

'Can you do shorthand and typing?'

'Of course,' she snapped.

'The last three couldn't,' he said. 'One couldn't spell, another stammered when she answered the phone and the third dropped everything she touched.'

'They were terrified of you, you mean,' she said shortly. 'Who can blame them?'

His brow lifted. 'Me?'

'Don't put on that innocent tone with me, Ben. You put the fear of God into those unfortunate girls and now you're trying it on with me, but this time it won't work. I'm not scared of you.'

His eyes surveyed her unreadably. 'As I remember it, you are,' he said very softly, and her face ran with angry colour. She glared at him and didn't answer. Ben turned away with a shrug.

'How long have you worked here?'

'Five years.'

He swung on his heel, staring at her. 'Five?' Her colour deepened and he said slowly. 'I see ...' and she wondered exactly what he saw but had no intention of asking.

Looking down, she tapped her pencil on her pad. 'I'm ready when you are.'

'Oh, put the thing away,' he said irritably. 'You don't imagine I'm going to have you working for me?'

'Why not?'

'Don't play the innocent with me. You know very well why not.'

She opened her eyes wide, her face cool. 'I'm quite capable, I assure you, and it won't bother me that you're my stepbrother.'

It was something she had never considered before,

and the relationship was so novel an idea that she found herself smiling.

'Take that smirk off your face,' Ben said sharply. 'What's funny?'

She remembered their last meeting and her eyes filled with savage laughter. 'You,' she said, because now she saw what had happened between them in an ironic light and they had both behaved absurdly. The whole thing had been a farce and in the clear light of day five years later she felt immune to him, and the relief was inexpressible. She could have shouted with it. He had haunted her and now she was free.

His eyes narrowed on her face for a moment, then he turned away and walked into his bedroom, coming back a moment later wearing an expensively tailored waistcoat which fitted his waist like a second skin, giving him a balletic elegance which irritated her. She did not want to be aware of his physical attraction now.

He stood there, fitting cufflinks into his shirt-sleeves, his black head bent, and Joanne could not take her eyes off him. Lifting his head, he said briskly, 'Right, let's get down to work, shall we? This morning I'll dictate to you. I want to test your speed and accuracy. If you're satisfactory, I'll use the dictaphone later. It saves time.' Without a pause he picked up a sheaf of letters from a table and began to dictate a series of letters in reply. Her fingers flew over the pad as she took them down. He was deliberately speaking very fast and she knew it, but she made no protest, merely stretching her own abilities to keep up with him. If he could keep it up so could she.

When he stopped at last she took a deep breath and

fixed a calm expression on her face. 'That all?'

The calm question infuriated him. 'No,' he said sharply. 'I'll have some more letters for you later. I want those typed now.'

'Yes, sir,' she said, moving to the door.

'When you've done them, bring them here to be signed,' he told her. 'I'm going out now. I'll be back at noon after the first conference session.'

'Yes, sir.'

His teeth came together. 'Oh, get out!' he snapped, and she saw that he was at the end of his tether. Their meeting had been as much a shock to Ben as it had been to her. Beneath the hard mask he was faintly human, after all.

In the lift she relaxed, her limbs shaking as she released them from the iron hold she had been forced to maintain over them for the last half hour.

She had lied to herself when she said she was immune to Ben. She had forgotten how he could make her feel. Now she remembered, and it was like being in the grip of some relentless fever. She was shivering with it, violently convulsive. Over the past five years she had tried to exorcise him by rigid self-control. Now she felt as though she had been in one position for so long that her body was cramped, her blood supply cut off, making her numb. A sight of Ben had set the blood moving again and the pain and elation of it was terrifying.

She typed the letters without making a mistake. It was a feat of extreme caution. She concentrated all her attention on making them perfect, and when she had finished it was nearly noon and she was drained.

Ben opened the door to her wordlessly and she held out the folder of letters. 'Ready for signature.'

He took the folder and glanced through them, his eyes flickering over the pages expressionlessly. He bent over a table, signing them, then straightened and said, 'Thank you. Are you free this afternoon?'

'Yes, sir.'

'Can you sit in on the conference? I want some notes taken.'

'Yes, sir.'

'Then I'll see you at the conference room at two-thirty.' He turned his back and she said coolly,

'I thought you wanted to dictate some more letters, sir.'

'I've changed my mind,' he said, so she went out, closing the door carefully, although she felt like slamming it until the windows rattled.

Joanne went back to the agency and Erma excitedly demanded to know how she had got on. 'He is difficult?'

'I can manage him,' said Joanne, consciously ironic.

Sighing with relief, Erma said, 'What would I do without you?'

'Blow bubblegum at him,' Joanne smiled and Erma went into gales of laughter.

Joanne had a quick lunch in the staff restaurant and went up to the conference room at two-thirty promptly. Ben gave her a quick, cold glance, his eyes glinting as they ran over her from head to toe. She had learnt not to blush; five years had done that much for her. But she was not able to meet his stare without feeling her pulses flutter. He was wearing a formal dark suit with a blue-striped stiff shirt and a dark tie and he looked maddeningly sexy; even the sardonic cast of his dark features could not detract from the physical allure of his body.

The conference was boring. Joanne had sat in on dozens of them and this one was no different. Men talked like droning bees and she wanted to yawn, but she fixed a bright, interested expression on her face, and whenever Ben turned his head and muttered a comment to her she took it down rapidly as though it were the word of a prophet. Her notebook soon began to fill up. Ben was shrewd, ruthless, knowledgeable. Some of his comments were icy criticism, some dry dismissals of the views expressed, some statistical notes. Joanne found she could pick up every intonation in the low voice. Although he spoke softly she heard every syllable.

She watched his dark lashes flick up and down, saw the line around his eyes deepen or diminish, and knew that time had changed nothing. Ben lit a flame inside her. She watched him hungrily and her fingers shook.

She really had to do something about the way she felt. She despised herself for it.

'Get those typed up, will you?' he asked afterwards, and she nodded.

'Yes, sir.'

They stared at each other. Ben turned away and she watched him walk towards the lifts, noting how people turned to stare at him. He was still a man people watched.

That evening Ralph picked her up after work. Getting into his car outside the hotel she felt herself under surveillance and glanced around. Ben was standing on the steps watching her, his face blank. Their eyes met and Joanne gave him a brief, polite nod, then got into the passenger seat and Ralph started the car, leaning forward to kiss her.

'You're looking very charming,' he commented with satisfaction, and she glanced down at the white silk blouse and charcoal grey suit she was wearing. The secretaries all wore what was known as 'house' colours —grey and white, although they could wear any style they liked so long as it was smart and discreet.

'They're new,' she said, and Ralph smiled.

'I had noticed.' He always noticed what she wore. He had almost as much interest in her clothes as she had, liking to see her well dressed. Ralph liked his women to be presentable.

Her blouse had a neat roll collar and a frilled jabot which fell to her waist, giving her an eighteenth-century look. The suit had a pleated skirt, tight-fitting jacket and a tiny waistcoat to match. They had cost the earth, but she knew they suited her slender figure. With her black hair wound in a chignon on her neck she looked elegant in them.

Ralph took her to dinner and talked as they ate, smiling at her, but she didn't hear a word. Subconsciously she was aware of his quiet voice. She made vaguely agreeable noises when he paused, reacting more to his tone than to what he said, and Ralph appeared quite satisfied. 'I'm glad you agree,' he said, and she wondered with wry amusement what she had let herself in for.

She tried to concentrate on him, but her mind kept

pulling away to thoughts of Ben and she was furious with herself for being so weak. Hadn't he hurt her enough in the past? She would have to be a masochist to go back for more, but she knew she could not detach her mind from him.

When Ralph kissed her goodnight she stood placidly in his arms and he was quite contented. Ralph lacked passion. He thought it was slightly vulgar, bad form. A conventional man, he preferred his women to be docile and submissive without being demanding. He saw passion as a form of greed and in a way, Joanne thought, it was; that was what she felt for Ben, a devouring hunger, and it shocked her to admit it.

Next morning when she reported to Ben's suite she was surprised to find her father there. He smiled at her affectionately. 'Hallo, Joanne.'

Ben was dressed in his formal business clothes today and his dark eyes swept over Joanne's charcoal grey uniform with a lift of those thin brows.

'Nice to have met you,' her father said, turning to him, sounding calmly amiable. She wondered if he knew of Ben's relationship to Jeb Norris and supposed he must do, but it would barely interest him. Her father had completely got over Clea years ago. Her remarriage was a matter of no concern to him.

He smiled at Joanne again and went out, and Ben said, 'Five years doesn't seem to have brought you two closer together. It's a distant father-daughter relationship, isn't it?'

'We were apart for too long,' she said calmly. 'We were almost strangers when I came over here and we've come very little closer together since.'

'Yet you stay,' he commented, watching her shrewdly.

'Yes,' she said, 'I stay,' and saw no reason why she should expand on the flat statement, since it was none of his business.

'You're engaged, I gather,' he said.

Her father must have told him and she tensed defensively. 'Yes.'

'The fellow you were with last night?' he asked, watching her with those cold dark eyes.

'Yes.' Something dismissive in his tone pricked at her, but she kept all colour out of her voice, her face cool.

'In love with him?' The question was casual, his eyes moving across the suite as if he had very little interest.

'Why else would I be marrying him?' she asked tartly.

The eyes came back to her and a faint, dry smile touched his mouth. 'Any number of reasons,' he said. 'Women marry for different things ... security, affection, desperation.'

It was all of those things, she thought, but she wasn't going to let Ben guess that.

'Well, I'm marrying for love,' she lied, and her voice was certain, untroubled.

He pushed his hands into his pockets and rocked on his heels. 'Have you seen much of them since you came here?' He did not specify the 'them' he meant, but there was no need to, they both knew who he was talking about.

'I see them occasionally,' she said. 'They're in London now.'

He looked taken aback, and she saw that he had not known that.

'My father didn't tell you?'

'We were talking about different things,' he said. He paused. 'Are they here in the hotel?'

'They've leased an apartment for a short time,' she said. 'But they'll be dining here tonight ... I'm having an engagement party at the hotel for my father and his wife and Clea and Jeb.'

'How civilised,' he said coolly. 'I wish I could be a fly on the wall.'

That wouldn't be funny, she thought. Ben's presence would turn what promised to be a difficult evening into a total disaster. She glanced at her watch. 'Shouldn't we get down to work? The conference starts in a quarter of an hour.'

His mouth indented. 'I've left some dictation on the dictaphone. You can work on that this morning.' He lowered his eyes to the floor. 'Is it possible for you to work up here? I would like to have someone manning the phone.'

'The hotel answering service will take messages.'

'I want someone here,' he repeated coldly.

Joanne tensed with irritation at the tone. 'Very well, sir,' she said, dropping back into a formal relationship.

Ben walked to the door. 'Will you order lunch up here for me? Order some for yourself. 'I'll work through the lunch break.'

Thank you, she thought furiously. How considerate of you. Aloud she said, 'Yes, sir. What shall I order for you?'

'Steak and salad,' he said without thinking, then as

he pulled open the door glanced at her through those thick black lashes and said, 'And a good wine.'

When he had gone Joanne picked up the telephone and dialled room service. She ordered steak and salad for two with melon as a starter and deliberately chose the most expensive wine on their list.

He had left her a mass of work to get done. She worked solidly all morning and had just finished when he came back at twelve. One of the porters had brought up her typewriter and arranged a desk in a good light. Ben stared at her across the suite and observed, 'You look very businesslike sitting there.'

'I am very businesslike,' she snapped.

He came over and picked up the folder of work, glancing through it, while she sat with her hands on the typewriter, not looking at him.

'Efficient,' he said, and there was mockery in his voice.

She glanced at him. 'I ordered the lunch for one o'clock. Is that satisfactory?'

'Fine,' he said, and before she knew what he meant to do he had leaned over and deftly undone the pins in her hair, letting it tumble around her astonished face. 'That's better,' he said coolly. 'I don't like it worn up.'

'What the hell do you think you're doing?' she asked angrily. 'Give me back my pins!'

He dropped them into the wastepaper basket beside the desk.

Joanne stared at them, biting her lip. Standing up, she bent to retrieve them and Ben's fingers closed around her wrist. 'No,' he said.

She straightened, glaring at him. 'I can't work with my hair in my eyes.'

'I'll brush it out for you,' he said, putting a hand to the full, dark waves of it as it fell around her flushed face.

'Don't touch me!' she snapped, pulling back, and there was open fear in her voice.

His hand fell away. He stared into her face. 'Wear it down from now on,' he said, turning away, 'when you're working for me.'

She drew a hard breath. 'Yes, sir,' she said bitingly.

Ben sat down on the edge of the desk, swinging his leg, his eyes on her face. 'Do you live in the hotel?'

'No.'

'Got a flat?'

'Yes.'

His eyes narrowed and a smile touched his mouth. 'Monosyllabic, aren't you?'

'You said you wanted to work through the lunch break,' she reminded him. 'That's why I'm here ... to work.'

'I'm paying you to do what I ask,' he said, unmoved by her sarcasm.

Joanne did not trust him. She sat down behind the typewriter as though it were a wall of defence. What was Ben up to now?'

'Does your fiancé share the flat?' he asked, and her cheeks burnt angrily.

'No!'

'Not your lover, then?' He swung his leg, staring at the polished black tip of his shoe.

'No,' she said, her voice shaking with the anger she was reining in, and her hands clenched in her lap.

'Have you had any?'

She would like to hit him, her hands gripped tightly to stop herself from jumping up and slapping him across the cold, sardonic face.

'That's my business,' she snapped, hoarse now with the effort to stop herself from losing her temper.

His eyes lifted sharply from his contemplation of his shoe and she met their stare angrily.

In the silence that followed the floor waiter knocked at the door and she went and opened it to let him into the suite. Ben walked to the window and stood there, his shoulders thrown back, his hands in his pockets, staring out at the London skyline.

When the waiter had gone Joanne asked coldly, 'Shall we eat now?'

Ben turned. 'Why not?' He sat down and looked at the melon. 'Very cooling,' he drawled, flicking a look at her hot cheeks.

She wondered what the waiter had thought, seeing her open the door with her hair loose around her pink face and no doubt a wrought-up look in her eyes.

Ben began to tell her about the conference and she listened as intently as though she were fascinated because at least it kept them off dangerous ground. He re-filled her glass whenever she reached halfway level and she lost count of the amount of wine she was drinking, but by the time they had reached the coffee she was feeling as though she were drifting on air, her head cloudy.

Ben watched her through lowered lids and she looked

back at him with stark awareness. The wine had lowered her resistance level. Her inhibitions were dissolving and she was alarmed by the rapid beating of her pulses.

'I'm never going to be able to work this afternoon,' she said. 'You must have a very clear head.'

'The afternoon session today isn't very important,' he told her. 'I'll skip it.'

That increased her alarm. His eyes were moving over her lazily and she was enjoying the way he looked at her, and that was dangerous. She wished she could force her way out of the heady haze the wine had invoked, but she was too languid.

Ben stood up, his hand pulling her to her feet, and she knew perfectly well that she was crazy, but when his dark eyes stared down into her face she leant against him as if she were too weak to stand alone, and waited for the touch of his mouth.

He did not kiss her, though. He watched her, his face unreadable. 'How much damage did I do, Joanne?' he asked, and for a long moment she stared at him in bewilderment, her face blank.

'That night on the yacht,' he added, seeing her lack of comprehension, and the reminder threw her back five years. She was wrung with pain, and she looked away, all the colour draining from her face; the warm, lazy feeling the wine had given her gone in a flash.

She had to answer him, but for a moment she couldn't make herself speak, then she summoned the will power from somewhere and looked back at him brightly, a smile pinned to her mouth.

'None,' she said. 'I got away, remember?' And she

made it sound like a joke, something meaningless.

Ben was watching her intently. 'You preferred to drown rather than let me make love to you,' he said lightly as if carrying on the joke.

'Sorry,' she said, still smiling.

He put his hand on her cheek and she felt each separate fingertip caress her skin and the nerves beneath her skin seemed to leap in response. 'Hadn't we better do some work?' she asked him in that bright voice which seemed to have no connection with herself.

He continued to stroke her face delicately, his eyes watching her. 'You astonished me when you jumped,' he said. 'Although you were making a noisy protest, when I got you in my arms your responses were passionate.'

The smile withered on her mouth. If she had spoken she would have lost her temper, so she clenched on unspoken fury, her eyes dark with it.

'I told myself I was dreaming it,' said Ben in that calm voice. 'But it flashed through my mind that you might be in love with me.'

'Why, you ...' Her angry outburst was smothered as his mouth came down on her own, hardening and searching, coaxing her lips to part for him.

His hands held her waist without pressure and she kissed him back, feeling the urgency running through her body until she was dazed with it.

She would never have had the strength to call a halt, but Ben did, he drew away and Joanne merely stood there, trembling, because she had lost control of her senses and she would have let him take anything he wanted.

He tilted her head again and she looked at him blindly. 'Now tell me the truth,' he said. 'How much damage did I do that night?'

He was asking her to admit she had been in love with him five years ago, that he had hurt her unbearably. He expected her to complete the humiliation he had achieved five years ago. She stared back at him and her temper flared bitterly.

'You behaved like a bastard,' she said. 'But that was your problem. I forgot you without any difficulty. I've barely remembered you since the last time I saw you.'

His eyes held mocking laughter. 'So I saw,' he said, and his glance dropped to her mouth. She turned to go and he caught her shoulders. 'I should have taken you five years ago,' he said. 'It would have got it out of our systems.'

'You make it sound quite hygienic,' she bit out.

'You've been in my bloodstream ever since,' he said conversationally, his features enigmatic, and her heart turned over as if he had said he loved her, although what he really meant was that they had begun something that night which lay unfinished between them and they both knew it. Unsatisfied desire could be as potent as love, and even though he was filled with hate for her and her mother, he had desired her.

She shook free of his grip and walked to the door a little unsteadily. 'It's all in the past, anyway,' she said, opening the door.

As she closed it she heard his voice ask softly, 'Is it, Joanne?' and she almost ran away from there, falling into the elevator as if she were running from a dangerous enemy, and in a way she was, because beneath

Ben's formal business persona he was still the hard, antagonistic man who had wanted to destroy Clea and would have used any weapon he could lay his hands on, even another human being.

CHAPTER SEVEN

SHE went down to the secretarial agency and told Erma she had a headache. Her flushed face and hectic eyes were convincing. Erma looked at her in concern. 'But tonight is your engagement party! This is sad.'

'If I may go home and rest for a few hours, it may go away,' Joanne explained, and Erma at once agreed. Joanne paused at the door, her eyes veiled.

'If the man in the Napoleon Suite wants me, send one of the other girls,' she said. Let Ben annoy someone else for a change, she thought, escaping.

In her flat she wandered restlessly around trying to calm her mind. Ben's lovemaking had caught her off balance. She had not expected it, and now that the effect of the wine had worn off she was furious with herself for having lost control. She should have seen that coming, but his coolness earlier had lulled her into a state of complacency. When she first saw him she remembered thinking that he should wear a label warning that he was dangerous.

She dressed for the party with a sense of premonition. It could be a stormy evening. Fasten the seat belts, she told herself, as she stared into the mirror. God knew what Clea would do. And after being in Ben's arms, Joanne was facing the fact that a lifetime spent with

Ralph had lost all its appeal. Safety and sanity might be wiser choices, but passion had a stronger pulling power.

She had to reason with herself, to remind herself of all the advantages Ralph could offer her. The marriage would suit both of them perfectly. Ralph did not want a passionate woman. He wanted a wife who would be cool, collected, elegant. He lived by a code of ethics based on good manners and good sense, and passion denied both. Ralph would never have tried to wreck anyone's life, as Ben had. He would be shocked to the core if she ever told him what Ben had tried to do to her, and he was right—of course he was right. Ben had behaved barbarously. She looked at herself in the mirror, seeing the sleek dark sweep of her black hair, the calm face, the slender lines of her body in the cream dress she wore, and that reflection mocked her memories of the night five years ago when Ben came close to destroying her. She looked too cool, too remote, for it to have been possible.

'You look wonderful,' said Ralph when he picked her up, and again she told herself wryly that she was doing him no injustice in marrying him without loving him, since he was certainly not in love with her. He would flinch away if she offered him love in any form other than that docile submission which he took for love. He was really extraordinarily like her father, but even her father had had his moment of pure madness. He had flung his bonnet over the windmill for Clea, and regretted it ever since.

They met the others in the bar, arriving to find a stilted little conversation going on between them. Jeb gave Joanne a wink surreptitiously. Her father was look-

ing uncomfortable, Angela faintly irritable. At a glance
Joanne saw that Clea had come along in mischievous
mood. Bright-eyed as a child at a Christmas Party, she
was giving John Ross flirtatious little glances from under her lashes. He was ignoring them, but Angela was
not; she was masking her anger, but it was a struggle.
Angela was too well-mannered to slap Clea's face, but
that was how it might end up if someone didn't do
something soon.

Joanne slid herself between her father and mother,
linking a hand through both their arms. 'A real family
party,' she said, smiling at Jeb and Angela at the same
time. 'I'm very lucky, having four parents.'

Angela looked uncertain about that, but Jeb lifted his
glass to her in a silent toast, his eyes warm.

'Darling, you look so pretty,' said Clea, and gave
Ralph a warm smile, approving of his good looks, his
way of dressing, his solid manners. 'Doesn't she look
sweet, Ralph?'

'Charming,' he agreed, smiling at Joanne. 'I'm very
proud of her.' He leaned over and kissed her lightly on
the mouth. 'And I'm very happy that she's going to
marry me.'

Clea was smiling as she turned and the smile
withered on her mouth. Jeb's brows drew blackly together and he turned, too, staring as she did at the door
into the bar.

Ben stood there, his dark face sardonic and hard to
read, the same arrogant mask he had worn when he
first came to Clea's villa. His eyes stopped on Clea who
stared at him warily. There was a silence while he ab-
sorbed the alteration five years had made. Clea would

never be ugly. She would never be less than striking. Joanne was sure she would make a beautiful old woman one day. But she would never again make the moon fall out of the sky and crowds fall silent in reverence as she passed.

Clea was not a fool. She could read the fleeting expression of incredulous pity which passed over his face. Joanne moved nearer to her, watching her uneasily. Jeb walked forward, offering his son his hand, and Ben slowly took it.

Joanne put an arm around her mother's shoulders and Clea, startled, looked round at her. 'In that shade of blue you look like a Madonna,' Joanne told her, and it was true. It was the shade which had always been Clea's favourite.

Distracted as a child, Clea looked down at it complacently. 'It's new,' she confided.

'Paris?'

'London,' said Clea, amused and pleased. 'There's a new young designer who can come up with some fabulous designs.'

Angela leant over towards them. 'Triccoli?' she asked eagerly, and Clea gave her a little smile.

'Do you visit his salon?'

Angela looked wistful. 'I wish I could afford it. I love clothes, but I have to watch my budget.'

Angela was fascinated by the secrets of Clea's life style. She envied her the clothes, the stars she knew, and now that Clea's attention had left John Ross, Angela was amiable towards her, eager to ask her questions and exchange views of clothes. Clea was famous and Angela saw her as a status symbol; she had a head-hunter's eagerness to collect Clea to display to her friends.

Ralph asked Joanne, 'Who is that?' staring at Ben.

'Oh, just my stepbrother,' she said lightly.

Ben glanced across at them with a glint in his dark eyes. She met the glance squarely, head up. He drew Jeb across towards them and Jeb introduced him to Ralph, who gave him a firm handshake and a friendly, faintly respectful smile. 'You run Norris Electronics now,' he said. 'That must be a tough job.'

Ben inclined his head, his dark eyes probing Ralph's good-looking, stolid face. Joanne could see that he was curious about Ralph. He wanted to know what made him tick and, Ben being Ben, it would not take him long to find out.

What was he doing here?

She looked at Jeb warily and Jeb's eyes were watchful. She wondered if Ben's appearance here tonight had troubled Jeb. It was troubling her. Why had he come? Had he some plan in mind? He seemed to be behaving with suspicious friendliness and she did not trust him an inch.

'I gather this is a celebration tonight,' said Ben, looking across at her.

'Yes,' Ralph said, smiling at her. 'Our engagement party.'

'When's the wedding?'

Ralph laughed. 'Oh, give us time,' he said. 'We're in no rush.'

Ben's dark eyes mocked Joanne across the little circle and she faced him with rising irritation. He was here to make trouble; she was certain of it.

'Oh, you want to get the girl into bed as soon as possible,' Ben said, grinning. 'Someone might run off with her if you don't.'

Ralph laughed complacently and she saw that he felt there was no chance of that. He was sure of her. He had taken her measure by the way her father's family talked of her. She was twenty-six and unmarried, and Ralph did not think there was any possibility that he would lose her. She had been on the shelf when he came along. Ralph was doing her a favour in taking her off it and he thought she must see that.

Jeb handed her a drink and she sipped at it, her eyes on her glass, while Ralph monopolised Ben's company. Jeb had relinquished control of the giant electronics firm to travel around with Clea. He was a king in exile. Ben was the king who wore the crown and Ralph respected him for the money and power he controlled.

John Ross had gone off to warn the head waiter that they would be one extra for dinner. He came back and smiled at Ben. 'Glad you could make it.'

Joanne saw from the look they exchanged that it was to her father that she owed Ben's appearance here tonight. Goodness knows how, but Ben had talked her father into inviting him, perhaps under a pretence of ending a family feud. On the surface that was what he was doing. He was talking to his father with every appearance of friendship and Jeb was looking more and more at ease.

Joanne had never felt less at ease. Ben's presence was a constant thorn in her side.

They went in to dinner in a little troupe, laughing and talking. Joanne sat between Ralph and her mother and could, by restricting her angle of vision, see nothing of Ben, but she could hear his voice however hard she tried not to, and she was certain he was pitching it for her ears.

'How long have you known Joanne?' he asked Ralph, and Ralph sounded vague as he answered, as though he were not sure.

'Oh, quite a while.' He paused long enough for courtesy and then asked Ben some questions about his firm. Ben parried them, his tone cool, half-bored, but Ralph was undeterred by his lack of real response. He talked about profit margins and annual growth rates, and Joanne distinctly heard Ben yawn.

Jeb leaned over the table and said softly to her, 'Ben is finding your fiancé heavy weather.' Jeb made no secret of the fact that he thought Ralph a dead bore. Ben's apparent agreement with him seemed to be amusing him, and his eyes were twinkling as he grinned at her.

She glanced across the dining-room and found with a shock that she could see Ben's arrogant head reflected in a gilt-framed mirror opposite. She watched him, wishing she could hate him, wishing she knew why he was here tonight.

Ralph asked him another elaborate question and Ben answered him flatly, his voice carrying a cool note which was a put-down, but it had no effect on Ralph. Joanne thought in sudden shock: Ralph is thick-skinned, and she had never known it before. She had never watched him in contact with a stronger, more able mind and seen him fumbling to prise it open as though it were an oyster which he suspected bore a hidden pearl.

They all went up to her father's private suite for the coffee. Ralph made his threatened speech over it. He had drunk far too much wine with the meal and his words rambled, grew hectoring. Joanne looked down at her linked hands with a flushed face. Once she looked up and met Ben's stare.

She looked at him with hostility, as though it was his fault. He was making Ralph look ridiculous to her, and she was furious with him. Merely by being in the same room, Ben outshone Ralph, and Joanne wished him on the other side of the world.

Ralph came over to kiss her and slide his ring on her finger. She was angry enough to put her arms round his neck and kiss him harder than she would otherwise have done, and Ralph looked surprised. He sat down next to her on the sofa and put an arm around her waist. Everyone talked cheerfully, drinking their coffee. Clea and Angela were still hard at it, swapping gossip stories about famous people and sighs of ecstasy over clothes. Angela was openly surprised to find Clea so easy to like, but women always did seem surprised by it. They expected something more feline, more offhand, and Clea was childlike and direct.

John Ross and Jeb were getting on like a house on fire. They had a lot in common, apart from Clea. They both played golf and it soon transpired that this was a cementing ground for an eternal friendship. They passed from polite chat into intensely excited talk of famous matches they had seen, grounds they had played on, holes they had made in one.

Ben lounged back in an armchair and Ralph talked to him across the room, still holding Joanne's waist. Ben's face was unreadable, but Joanne felt nervous sitting there with Ralph's hand below her breast. Once or twice Ben glanced at it and then up at her face, and each time her heart dropped as though she were in a lift which suddenly went down.

'A brandy?' her father asked Ralph, turning from the decanter, and Ralph suddenly stood up, looking pale.

'Afraid I must be off,' he said abruptly. 'I have a headache.'

Joanne stood up too. 'Yes, I must go, myself,' she said lightly. 'I have to work tomorrow.'

'You can't both go,' Ben said coolly. 'After all, that will spoil the party.'

'Yes, yes,' said Ralph, half stumbling to the door. 'Stay, Joanne.' She would have followed him stubbornly, but Jeb caught at her hand and smiled at her.

'Stay and talk to me, Joanne.' She hesitated and he hissed conspiratorially, 'I fancy your fiancé has drunk a little too much, darling. Not tactful to follow him.'

She flushed and turned to sit down, freezing as she found Ben lowering himself on to the sofa in Ralph's place. He jerked her down, his hand round her wrist, and they looked at each other silently.

'So that's the man you plan to marry,' he said, and she heard sarcasm in his voice. 'My God! You could have done better than that, Joanne.'

'Ralph suits me,' she said, and he laughed.

'He'd bore you to death. Get into bed and he'll start giving you a projected graph of annual growth rates.'

'Oh, shut up!' she snapped, driven beyond her limit.

He glanced at the others who were engaged in two separate conversations still, their voices rising noisily.

'An odd occasion,' he commented drily. 'They make a strange quartet.'

Joanne looked at him uneasily and he met her stare with a faint smile. 'Stop looking so edgy,' he told her. 'You've been eyeing me all night as if you suspected I had a stick of dynamite in my pocket.'

'Can you blame me?'

He shrugged. 'I'm five years older, five years wiser. Even hatred wears out in the end.'

And love, she thought, does that wear out? Oh, God, I hope so. Ben looked into her eyes as though he could read her mind and a hard smile lifted the edges of his mouth.

She looked away, pleating her skirt with nervous fingers. Ben took her hand and inspected her ring with an impassive face.

'Expensive,' he said, handing it back as if bored with it.

The diamond flashed under the lights and she moved her hand, watching it.

'But tasteless,' Ben added, and she glared at him.

'Keep your opinions to yourself if you can only be rude about it!'

'Not rude,' he said. 'Frank.' His dark eyes stayed on her face. 'I'd buy you sapphires,' he said. 'The colour of your eyes.'

'I wouldn't let you buy me a bag of crisps,' she snapped.

'Have you ever told Ralph that I offered to buy you

a diamond bracelet for a few nights in Paris?' he asked coolly.

She gave him a look which should have gone through his shoulder blades. 'No, I haven't. Do you think I go around boasting of it?'

'I don't know,' he said. 'I expect he would consider it flattering that I made the offer. It puts a price on you, and Ralph understands that. Think how much he would respect you for having refused.'

'Go to hell!' she said, and got up. Her voice had been slightly too fierce and Jeb turned to stare at her flushed face. She mumbled a flurried goodnight and almost ran out of the room. Ben came after her and she turned on him in the corridor. 'Will you leave me alone?'

'Not until I've got what I want,' he said casually, and her colour deepened to a hectic red.

'You bastard!'

He caught her hand as it flailed up to hit him and held it down without effort, twisting it behind her back, jerking her towards him so that their faces were inches apart.

'You're too passionate for that cold fish you've hooked,' he said lazily. 'You'll terrify him.' His eyes glinted. 'You terrify me at times, Joanne. All that fire under that cool little face ... a man could get burned alive.'

'Don't tempt me,' she retorted scathingly.

His eyes mocked. 'I'm going to,' he promised. 'Day and night.'

He was tempting her now and she was torn between a desire to go into his arms and a desire to knock him from one end of the corridor to the other. She compromised by twisting out of his grip suddenly and walking off with her head in the air. She thought he might follow her, but he just stood there and laughed, and she could hear the sound of that laughter even in the elevator taking her down to the hotel foyer.

Jeb rang her later that night. Joanne had a terrible feeling of disaster as she recognised his voice, but he only wanted to talk. 'Why do you think Ben came?' he asked her, and she said with a faint sigh,

'I've no idea. Why do you?'

Jeb sighed. 'I hope because he's finally come to terms with my marriage, but with Ben you can never be sure.'

'He said even hatred wears out in the end,' she offered, although as he said, how could you believe a word Ben said?

'He seemed different,' Jeb admitted. 'More relaxed, easier . . .'

He was enjoying himself, she thought, but she was not going to make Jeb more worried by telling him precisely how Ben had been amusing himself.

'We'll just have to wait and see,' Jeb sighed before he rang off. His sense of threat from Ben did not make it any easier for Joanne to get to sleep that night. She lay awake for hours, twisting and turning on her pillows, and in the morning she felt grey and drawn.

Ben rang for her a few moments after she got to work and when she went into his suite he eyed her consideringly. 'You were late this morning. Sleep badly?'

'Overslept,' she said tightly. 'Shouldn't you be in the conference? It started ten minutes ago.'

'I waited to see you,' he said. 'I worked late last night. I want all these tapes transcribed.'

She looked at the pile of them and nodded grimly. He looked as impervious as ever and if he had worked late it did not show.

'I'll be back at twelve,' he said. 'We'll have a working lunch again.'

Oh, no, we won't, she thought, eyes defiant. Aloud she said, 'I'm sorry, I have a date.'

'Cancel it,' he said, unmoved.

'I'm afraid I can't.'

'There's no such word,' he said. 'Cancel it.' He went to the door and she followed him, arguing.

Ben grinned at her. 'I'll see you at twelve. Keep the place till then.'

When he had gone she swore for a moment with a fluency she had not known herself capable of, then she threw herself into the work with a grim air.

He had not told her to order lunch. He had presumably meant her to, but since he had not specifically ordered it, she deliberately did not do so.

When he came back she indicated the neat pile of work on the desk. 'All done,' she said. 'I must go now, I'm afraid.'

He caught her arm as she walked past. 'We're lunching on the river,' he said.

'I told you...'

He put a hand over her mouth and her eyes threw rage at him over the top of it.

'What can I do to you in public?' he asked lightly.

Joanne fumed but gave in because she could not see that he could do anything.

Ben took her to a barge on the river Thames under the slanting green leaves of a willow and they ate fine

French cooking and talked lightly while a tape played Simon and Garfunkel in the background over and over again. 'Do you think they only have one tape?' she asked him, sipping her wine.

'They know I like it,' he said.

She was startled. 'You do?'

'Don't you?' He looked as if he minded whether she did or not, and she gave him a sudden, melting smile.

'I love it,' she said, and knew she would never forget the soft ripple of the guitar music mingling with the sound of the river and the whisper of the wind in the willows.

Ben put a hand across the table and pulled out one of the pins in her hair. 'Let it down,' he said, and the softness of his tone was hypnotic. She found herself obeying like an automaton.

He flicked the black strands with one finger. 'Now you look the way I like you to look.'

I'm crazy about you, she thought, lowering her lashes to hide the look in her eyes. He had taken off his dark tie and undone the top button of his shirt. The dark brown of his throat argued with the formal business suit. The wind lifted his black hair and he raked it down with one hand, smiling at her.

They took their time and Joanne did not want the meal to end. After their coffee they walked along the riverbank and listened to the slap of the water on moored boats. She saw a flash of brown as a water rat flopped down into the water and ripples spread out as it swam away.

Ben was whistling one of the tunes from the tape under his breath. He really did like it, she thought, and glanced at him sideways, catching his eyes on her.

He stopped under an oak tree and pushed her gently against the rough trunk. His hands slid into her long loose hair and he stared at her face.

'Give him his ring back,' he said. 'I'm not going to let you marry him.'

She did not want him to talk. Her mind was hazily set on other things. She looked at the strong brown muscles of his throat and then at his mouth, and her eyes were languid. She was not listening and he could see it.

He put one of his wandering hands against her cheek and bent. She met his mouth hungrily, melting into his arms with a faint sigh. The pressure of unsatisfied desire built up rapidly in her. She groaned, her arms around his back, her hands climbing to the nape of the strong neck, feeling the bristle of his hair against her fingertips.

His lean body, lowered against her and she gasped, her hands tightening on him. He pressed down on her, moving against her, and she had no defences against how he was making her feel. She knew he had to be aware of the slow shudder passing through her. His hands stroked over her breasts and her nipples hardened under their touch. He was setting off exploding signals all along her nervous system as though he were a sapper laying mines, his long hands moving expertly, knowing precisely what they were doing.

He lifted his head and looked down into her hectically flushed face. 'I'm not making love to you for the first time on a towpath,' he said thickly. 'Have dinner with me tonight.'

The unspoken rider hung in the air between them and she gave no sign of protest or rejection, just shaking her head. 'I've promised to have dinner with Ralph.'

'Tell him to drop dead,' Ben told her.

She laughed huskily. 'Poor Ralph! I can't.'

'You're not marrying him,' he said, and he was not asking her, he was telling her, and he did not doubt that she would break the engagement.

'I have to talk to him,' she said, admitting by her tone that she was not going to marry Ralph. It had been a stupid thing to do, getting engaged to a man she did not love, merely because everyone expected her to do so.

'Afterwards?' he asked, looking at her mouth in a way which made her light-headed.

'Don't rush me, Ben,' she begged. 'Please!'

'Rush you?' He sounded drily ironic. 'I've waited five years. Do you call that rushing you?'

'Please,' she said again, putting her hands on his chest palm down, her fingers spread across his shoulders.

He groaned. 'Are you making me pay for what I did that night? I'm going out of my mind.' She did not need to hear him say that. His dark eyes were looking at her in a way which elated and excited her.

'Very well,' he said menacingly. 'I'll wait for you until tomorrow. But you'll pay for it then, I promise you.'

Joanne smiled into his eyes. 'Will I?' Her blue eyes teased him and he kissed her hard before he walked her back to his car.

'I don't want to see that ring on your hand again,'

he said as they parted, and she solemnly took it off and dropped it into her handbag. Ben's dark eyes sparked triumphantly at her as he drove away leaving her outside her flat feeling dazed.

When she told Ralph he was torn between anger and disbelief. He assured her it was bridal nerves. 'You'll regret the whole thing tomorrow,' he said, and she hoped to God he was wrong about the regret waiting for her tomorrow, but it would not be a regret for him, that much she knew for certain. She had drifted into this engagement with Ralph without any real volition and ever since she set eyes on Ben again she had known she was never going to go through with it. Giving herself to Ralph when she loved Ben would have been a form of adultery in her own eyes. It sickened her to think of herself in Ralph's arms.

'I'm sorry, Ralph,' she said, and he was tight-lipped.

'Why wait until tonight? Why not have told me yesterday before I'd made a fool of myself by giving you my ring publicly?'

'I'm sorry,' she said again, and tried to think of some other way of apologising. 'I made a mistake.'

'So did I, it seems,' he said coldly, and his pride was hurt. He was furious with her. He looked at her with distaste. 'I suppose you've got better prospects?' he asked, and there was an ugly tone in his voice suddenly.

She was bewildered. 'What do you mean?'

'Oh, come on,' he said shortly. 'Ben Norris is a richer catch than I am!'

She had not breathed Ben's name to him, so how had he caught on to that? She looked at him in surprise, wondering if he had noticed something in the way they looked at each other last night.

'You'll be lucky if you hook him,' Ralph added and she wondered how she had ever imagined that he could not be vulgar. 'He's a very experienced fish and cleverer anglers than you have tried to land him.'

She looked at him expressionlessly and knew she did not like him at all. He had a very unpleasant mind.

After that nasty little interlude she did not feel like going to her empty flat and trying to get to sleep with a mind and heart full of Ben. She had to see him, to touch him, because the moments by the river were eating at her and she knew she could not wait until tomorrow. She had to be in his arms tonight.

When she got to the hotel the porter looked curiously at her and she smiled as she walked into the elevator. She tapped on the door and after a few moments Ben opened it. He was in his dressing-gown and there was a wary, startled look on his face as he saw her.

Joanne flushed, feeling suddenly stupid for having come. 'Do I come in or not?' she asked him, wishing she had stayed in her flat.

He seemed to hesitate, a frown on his face. Another guest came down the corridor behind her, so she walked in past Ben and then stopped dead, her whole body tensing with a terrible realisation.

He closed the door and turned to her with his hands thrust into his dressing-gown pockets. 'I thought you were dining with Ralph,' he said flatly.

She turned on her heel and walked over to the bedroom door. Ben sprang after her, muffled words on his lips, but she had reached it before he got to her. She flung it open and looked across the bedroom at Clea.

She rose from the bed in a low-cut blue evening dress, looking distraught and frantic. 'Joanne!'

Joanne looked at Ben, her eyes searing, then she turned and ran out of the suite. He came after her saying harshly, 'Don't jump to conclusions, Joanne. I can explain...'

'I bet you can,' she said bitterly. The elevator was still at the floor. She got into it and Ben tried to drag her out. She was inspired with a maniac strength conferred by a jealousy which made her almost homicidal. She threw him back with both hands and in the few seconds he was off balance the door closed and the elevator headed down for the foyer.

She stared straight ahead, her eyes burning. The porter looked at her as she walked out. She took one of the taxis waiting outside and stared out at the neon lights of the great city as though they were the lights of hell itself.

Back at her flat she wrote a short letter to her father, packed a case and left almost immediately. London was quietly deserted. The air was chill. Joanne got a train in the grey dawn light after a night spent waiting in the echoing railway station, stared at curiously by porters. Her mind was goading her all the time, playing over the images of the two of them in that suite, and she knew that nothing Ben had done to her in the past could equal what he had done to her tonight.

CHAPTER EIGHT

SHE barely knew what she was doing. Like someone in a dream, she got off the train and walked out of the station, standing there in the busy street, dazed and empty, her case on the pavement beside her.

Her wandering eye took in a single-decker bus and the name leapt out at her. Grenoch ... she had once stayed there for two weeks with her father and Angela. Whenever she could escape from the placid routine of their idea of a seaside holiday, she would walk off along the cliffs, staring at the grey-blue sea, watching it smash violently against the rocks, white foam flying upward in the wind. The turmoil of the elements had excited her. She picked up her case and started towards the bus instinctively, following some secret prompting.

They took a winding, narrow lane through wind-blown green fields. She caught snatches of talk from the other passengers, their soft, burring voices muffled by the roar of the engine. 'So I said to her ...' The woman speaking laughed as she finished the anecdote and her companion laughed in response, but Joanne heard it without smiling, feeling remote from all human beings, isolated, marooned on a desert island of the emotions.

All her life she had walked in the shadows while her beautiful mother stood in the sun. She felt cheated, betrayed. Clea had had so many lovers and admirers. They had flocked to worship at her feet. Yet she had taken Ben lightly, casually, out of a consuming vanity which needed to be fed by having conquered him.

The bus pulled to a juddering halt in a tiny village street. Joanne got up without even needing to think about it and made her way to the doors. The other passengers watched her curiously. She climbed down and watched the bus sail on. The street was empty, silent. She looked around in that slow, dazed fashion and then walked with her case to the top of Church Lane. She remembered it vividly, the cobbled little street falling steeply to the harbour, a channel at each side of it along which rain ran to drain into the sea. The spire of the tiny church reached up to the sky, the foot of the church buried in a sea of gravestones, wedged close together, grass springing up between. A low wall round the churchyard fenced them in and from it one could stand and stare at the sea below, the rocks like jagged teeth showing through the leaden waves.

Joanne went to the same little hotel where she had stayed years ago with Angela and her father. There was a room vacant. She took it, and felt no surprise or relief. It seemed only what she had expected.

Alone in the room, she sat down on the bed and shivered, as though at the onset of a feverish cold.

After a few moments she lay down and closed her eyes. No thoughts ran through her head. She was dead, empty.

It was a week before she thought of writing to Milly. She felt no compunction in walking out on the others. She knew they would not truly miss her or worry about her, although her father might, from a sense of duty, wish she would let him know she was safe. Once he knew that, he could quieten his conscience and get on with his own life. That was all she was to him, a duty.

Milly, on the other hand, had given her affection and care throughout her life, and she knew Milly would be worrying.

She wrote to her briefly, carefully, saying she had felt the need to get away alone, asking her to tell nobody where she was, to keep the letter to herself.

Having been here a week, she began to wake up from her cold nightmare. Blood beat through her veins again. She saw what she was looking at, taking in the stark, powerful beauty of the Cornish coast with admiring eyes. She walked every day for hours, zipped up in a fur-lined parka, the hood giving her a pixie-like look. It helped her to wear her body out with walking. Exhausted, chilled and hungry, she returned each day and ate a good meal before going to her room and sleeping for hours like a log.

When she thought of Ben now it was with contempt and bitterness. Love had dried up in her. She felt untouchable, unreachable.

Her favourite walk was along the cliffs in the face of a howling gale, down a steep path, finding footholds where she could, into a tiny creek. A narrow river ran through it to the sea, embedded in rocks and grass and great, wind-tossed trees. She rarely found anyone else there. It was too remote for tourists, too difficult to reach by road and too dangerous by the cliff path. Several times she found her foot sliding away beneath her on the crumbling path and had to cling on frantically until she recovered her balance.

She was waiting now for a letter from Milly, sure

that she would write back. Under her frozen calm, she was hungry for news. What had happened after she ran out of Ben's suite? Was he still seeing Clea? Joanne knew that Milly would be aware of it, as she was aware of everything touching Clea. Jeb might be fooled; Milly never.

She came back from her walking one evening to meet Ben in the narrow street. She stopped dead, seeing him, and turned on instinct to walk away. He caught up with her, his hand seizing her arm.

'Let me go!' She thought of Milly with fury. How dare she betray her confidence like this?

'You've got to come back,' he said coolly.

'Oh, no,' she retorted, her teeth coming together. 'Oh, no!'

'Clea needs you,' he said.

She felt the blood beat in her temples. Her eyes swung to his face, rage and hatred in them. 'Clea has never needed anyone in her life.'

'She needs you now,' he said patiently.

She laughed, sarcasm in her voice.

'Jeb is ill,' he said.

Her face altered. Surprise and regret in it. 'I'm sorry. Is it serious?'

'Touch and go,' he said, grimacing.

'What's wrong?'

'A brain tumour,' he said.

Joanne winced. 'No!'

'He collapsed two days ago. They operated last night. He got through the operation, which was a miracle, but now we have to wait and see whether he has the physical strength to recover from it.'

'I'm sorry,' she said again, sighing. 'I like Jeb.'

He looked at her, the dark eyes searching her face, trying to read her mind. 'So you see why you've got to come back. Clea needs you. Jeb's illness has terrified her. She's like a lost soul. You must come and comfort her.'

A confused chaos filled Joanne's mind. She felt like screaming and fighting. She looked at him, white and hollow-eyed, saying nothing.

'Why didn't Milly write?' The question came out before she knew she had asked it.

'We weren't sure you would come.' Ben admitted that flatly.

She smiled acidly. 'No,' she said.

'But you must,' Ben said.

She looked at him without expression, then turned and walked to her hotel. He followed. 'Wait here,' she said, going into the little office. She paid her bill and went up to her room, packed her things. When she got back down she found him waiting.

'My car is outside,' he said, taking her case.

They drove in a heavy silence, islanded in their own thoughts. Joanne could almost hear his, she read the glances he gave her, tentative, shrewd looks which tried to read her mind.

'It wasn't what you thought,' he said at last.

'Forget it, Ben. There's no need for explanations. It isn't my business.' She stared out of the window with her head averted from him, the sleek black chignon wreathed at the back of her neck.

He glanced at it and then at her cheekline, the obstinate curve of her chin. 'You're going to hear the truth whether you want to or not.'

'I don't.'

'I'm aware of that,' he said curtly. 'You prefer being the injured party.'

She turned and her eyes hated him. 'I'm indifferent,' she said. 'After all, I've had years to get used to Clea's affairs. I lost count of her men while I was still at school. Enjoy it while you can, Ben—it won't last long.'

He pulled up with a screeching of tires and she shrank back into her seat. 'Stay away from me!'

'Never in this life,' he muttered through his teeth. 'But you needn't shake in your shoes just yet, Joanne. I'm not going to touch you, I'm just going to make you listen. I'm not driving all the way to London with you sitting there hating my guts.'

She sat up straight, her hands in her lap, her eyes averted. If he insisted on telling her some fairy tale to account for Clea's presence in his bedroom, then let him. She wouldn't believe a word of it. She had believed him once. Never again.

'She came to see me to talk about my father,' he said through his teeth. 'She suspected something was wrong with him. He was showing signs of failing eyesight, bumping into things which were on the edge of his sight, having strange swings of mood, tempers, inexplicable bursts of rage. Clea was worried and frightened, so she came to me.'

It could be true, but Joanne was not convinced. Clea had been too guilty when she walked into that bedroom. There had been a conscious, stricken look in her eyes.

'That's what she told you?' Her voice was biting.

'It's the truth!'

She shrugged. 'If you say so.'

Ben stared at her, his mouth held rigidly. 'My God, I'd like to shake you!'

'Shouldn't we get on? There's a long drive ahead of us.'

He started the car again and shot away, his head lowered, his eyes fixed on the road. For a while neither of them said anything, then he asked huskily, 'Why did you come that night?'

Joanne felt colour burn up her face. 'I forget,' she said shortly.

He laughed. 'I'll help you to remember later,' he said, and she could have hit him.

He drove her straight to the hospital at which Jeb was lying, waiting for the moment of decision. Milly and Clea sat together in a waiting room, side by side, like huddled birds on a washing line, their bodies hunched in grim resignation.

Milly looked up and Joanne saw the relief break through her grey face.

Clea turned her head slowly. Her violet eyes registered her daughter dully. Joanne knew as she saw the look in those still lovely eyes that her suspicions were true. Clea had gone to Ben that night with a deeper reason than a desire to confide her anxieties to him. Clea had been hurt by Ben's visible reaction to her own ageing. She had gone to him in one last attempt to recapture her vanished youth.

Slowly Joanne went to her. Clea watched her, almost shrinking, like a child who fears punishment.

Joanne crouched and put her arms around her and suddenly Clea was crying, weeping wildly, clinging to her. 'He's going to die,' she sobbed. 'Because of me.'

'No,' soothed Joanne, patting her shoulder. 'Jeb is too strong, he has a deep will to live. Jeb will come through this . . . if you're there when he wakes up, Clea. You have to be with him when he opens his eyes. You are what he'll live for.'

Clea did not stop crying. She could not, it seemed. The tears ran in rivers, and Joanne could not help thinking, in cynical amusement, that part of Clea's grief was for herself. She was shedding tears now for a multitude of reasons, not all of them to do with Jeb. She was facing too many hard facts at once and she did not have the spiritual strength to do so. Ben was right. Clea needed her, just as she needed Milly and Jeb, and Ben, and anyone who would support her. She was clinging ivy, winding its thin frail stem around anything that would hold it up.

Joanne went on patting her, stroking her, comforting her. Clea's body was ageing, but the mind within it was eternally childlike.

Ben reappeared some minutes later with a tray of tea. They all sat drinking it, speaking rarely. Clea vanished to wash her face and resume the smooth, pampered mask she showed the world. Milly laid a hand on Joanne's.

'Thank you for coming back.'

Joanne looked at her wryly. 'Why didn't you write and tell me?'

Milly met her eyes. 'I wasn't sure you would come.'

Joanne shrugged. 'I had to.'

Milly nodded. 'Yes, you had to,' she agreed. 'But I guessed you'd take some persuading.'

So she had sent Ben, and the perception behind that made Joanne wince. How many other people now knew how she felt about Ben?

'When Jeb collapsed, Clea fell to pieces,' Milly went on. Her face was rueful. 'I had my hands full with her, I can tell you. She was petrified. Death terrifies her, and she was certain he was dying. Clea isn't a tower of strength when anyone is ill. We'll have to nurse her as much as Jeb. She mustn't be allowed to make him gloomy with long faces.'

The doctor insisted that Clea must go and rest that evening. She had sat at the hospital ever since Jeb collapsed and the strain was showing on her.

Milly took her off to bed when they got back to the apartment they were renting. Ben wandered over to the sideboard and poured himself a double whisky without asking. Joanne asked tartly, 'May I have something to drink, please?'

'What do you want?' He turned and looked at her levelly.

'Gin and orange.'

'Coming up,' he said, pouring it. He came back and put the glass into her hand and she swallowed some quickly while he watched her from beneath the straight dark line of his brows.

'Did you think I'd succumbed to Clea's blandishments, Joanne, or that I was still trying to revenge my mother?'

She drank some more of the gin very fast. 'I really didn't care which.' What did it matter why he was with

Clea? That he was had been intolerable enough.

'I would have thought it mattered,' he said casually, as if the subject were purely academic. She finished her drink and got up and walked to the sideboard to pour herself another. Ben followed her and put a hand over her glass.

'You've had enough.'

'Will you mind your own business?'

'It is my business. I don't want you too tipsy to understand a word I'm saying.'

'Go to hell!'

Ben laughed, taking her slim shoulders, turning her to face him. 'My God, what a life I'm going to have with you!'

Joanne looked up into his face in shock and incredulity. He put a hand to her cheek and stroked it gently.

'Five years ago when I got you on that yacht I told myself I was doing it out of revenge, but it was a lot more complicated than that ... I wanted you badly, Joanne.'

The blue eyes widened and then fell. Ben watched her with an intent face.

'I treated my mother pretty badly while she was alive. I was too intolerant—adolescents often are. By the time I was beginning to feel any sympathy for her, it was too late ... she died before I had a chance to make it up to her.' He grimaced. 'I hated myself for that. It's never pleasant to hate yourself, so I conveniently transferred all my own guilt and self-contempt to Clea and my father. I found that easier to bear.'

She looked up at him searchingly. 'I'm sorry about

your mother, Ben. She must have been very unhappy.'

He nodded grimly. 'My father says she was already sick long before he met Clea, and I believe him now ... I wouldn't believe it when he first told me because I preferred my own version, but I believe him now. I've faced my own guilt and accepted it.' He looked down at her, his dark eyes unsmiling. 'I think I was sick myself when I met you five years ago. I'd been brooding over my mother's death for months. I came to France to revenge her.'

She nodded, watching him. His features had a sombre darkness which hurt.

'At first sight, Clea was so incredibly beautiful that I was knocked off balance, but she's shallow, Joanne ... no feelings.'

She shook her head. 'You're wrong. Clea loves Milly and Jeb.' As a child loves its parents, she thought, with selfish, cheerful certainty that they will always love it in return whatever it does.

He shrugged. 'Anyway, I went ahead with my plan to wreck what remained of her career. She was desperately eager to get backing for her new film and it never seemed to occur to her to be surprised that I should be ready to back it.'

Of course it wouldn't surprise Clea, she thought. Clea had been used to making men fall over themselves to do what she wanted.

Ben moved his hand and undid her chignon slowly, watching the heavy fall of the black hair with intensity. He moved his fingers through the strands. 'But there was you ... I had the idea you were about sixteen. You looked so damned young, and then you got out of that pool with your hair wet, shaking it, and I stared as if I'd never seen you before ... when Clea was around you seemed to melt into the wallpaper, but that morning I really looked at you and, my God! Joanne, I fancied you.'

She laughed at the wryness of his tone, blushing. She remembered the way he had deliberately moved into her path and she believed him. It had been there between them that morning, physical awareness, but she had been too inexperienced to be sure if she was reading the look in his eyes correctly.

'When you came to Lester's party in that red dress I couldn't take my eyes off you and I was furious with you for the way you were flirting with Sam Ransom.' He looked down into her eyes. 'He did kiss you, didn't he?'

'Yes,' she said, and Ben's mouth hardened.

'You were distracting him from Clea, weren't you? Clea was frightened of him—she told me so. He had some grudge against her and she was scared what he might write about her.'

'She's my mother,' Joanne said. 'Sam was angry with her and he could be very malicious in a bad mood.'

Ben's hand slid round her throat. 'So you soothed him down, did you? I ought to beat you for that. I was as jealous as hell.'

Her heart turned over and the blue eyes were wide with feeling. 'Were you, Ben?'

He kissed her and she put her arms around his throat and kissed him back meltingly. He put his face against her hair and groaned.

'When I kissed you myself later that night I was in a

black temper, but I couldn't get over the fact that I wanted you. I was confused. I could see I wasn't going to be able to follow through with my plan. My father had come to see to that. He didn't say so, but when we looked at each other I knew exactly why he was there ... he still cared for Clea, and he wasn't going to let me do a thing to her.'

Jeb was shrewd, Joanne thought, and he knew his son. 'In a way, you brought them together again,' she said. 'Jeb would never have come if he hadn't wondered what you were up to.'

Ben grimaced. 'That occurred to me later and I didn't find the idea very pleasing.' He grinned at her. 'It's easy to think of good reasons for doing something you badly want to do. I wanted you, so I told myself I would hurt Clea through you.'

And he had, she thought grimly. She had paid for five years. She looked down, pulling out of his arms, and Ben let her go, watching her.

'When you jumped overboard rather than let me make love to you, I was furious,' he told her. 'You caught my ego on the raw. I went off to Paris and spent a few crazy weeks trying to forget it ever happened.'

'You came to the wedding, though.'

'The newspaper gossip forced me to do that,' he shrugged. 'I wasn't going to be haunted by speculation about whether or not I'd ever been in love with Clea.' He laughed grimly. 'My God, I hated her! It was all I could do to be polite to her whenever I saw her.' He stared at her averted face, tracing the pure line of cheek and chin. 'I saw you at the wedding with Sam Ransom. You never looked at me once.'

She could have laughed aloud at that. She had watched him so intently and yet he had not been aware of it.

'I wanted to come over there and make you look at me,' he went on. 'You looked cool and untouchable in a blue dress and I wanted to pull your hair down, make you kiss me.'

'That would have caused some talk,' she said lightly.

'When I was going you finally looked at me,' he said, his hand under her chin, turning her face towards him. The dark eyes stared down at her. 'I felt two feet high. You looked at me with contempt and I walked out of there wanting to hit somebody.'

He had not shown it. He had looked impervious, and beneath her own calm manner she had been aching with love for him.

'I went back to work and I told myself I would forget you inside a month,' he said. 'When I opened the door of my suite and saw you five years later, I was shaken to find I'd never forgotten a thing. I was angry with myself, with you. You sat there taking dictation and I kept looking at your hair, at your legs, and I was going crazy.'

'You're a good actor, then. You never showed a thing.'

He grinned at her. 'That's a relief. I thought I might be obvious. You laughed at me at one point, and I went blind with rage.'

'Did I?' She could not remember. She only remembered the intense physical awareness she had been feeling.

'When I saw you getting into a car and saw the man driving it kiss you, I was knocked for six. That was when I realised I'd never get over the way I felt about you. I rang your father and he came up to see me next morning and I asked him about you. He told me you were getting engaged and I knew I had to stop it. I couldn't stand the thought of you with another man.' He looked at her passionately. 'I love you, Joanne. You've got to believe me.'

'I believe you,' she said soberly. 'But we can never have any sort of lasting relationship, Ben.'

'Like it or not, we've got one,' he said huskily.

She walked away and stood at the window. 'No,' she said in a quiet voice. 'There's too much against us.' She thought of Clea's guilty, worried face and winced. 'I don't just mean the past. The future, too. They've left us with a tangled web, Ben. I've neither the energy nor the desire to sort it out.'

'I'm not going to lose you,' he said harshly.

'You haven't got the option.'

'Only one thing matters,' he said, moving over to her. 'Do you love me?'

She turned her head away, not answering.

'Why did you come that night? Why did you rush out after seeing Clea without waiting to hear a word of explanation?'

'What was the point of staying? Or did you expect me to make up a cosy threesome in your bedroom?'

His eyes flashed furiously at her. 'I've told you ...'

'I didn't know what to believe,' she sighed. 'I judged on what I saw, on what I knew of Clea.'

'You jumped to conclusions, then.'

'So you say now. At the time, that was all I had to go on.'

'You stubborn little mule,' he muttered, shaking her.

'Let me go, Ben! You're going to leave bruises on me.'

'You've left bruises on me,' he said grimly. 'By God, you have, Joanne. When you ran out without listening to me, I felt as if you'd kicked me in the stomach. I knew damned well what you were thinking, and it wasn't a pretty picture.'

'I didn't find it too charming myself.'

'No,' he said, staring down into her face, his insistent gaze bringing a hot flush to her cheeks. 'And that brings us back to my first question: why did you come that night?'

She turned her head away to escape his eyes, but he forced it round, his hands framing her face. 'Tell me,' he said softly, watching her.

She swallowed. 'You know very well why.'

'Tell me,' he said.

'You devil,' she whispered.

His eyes dropped from her own to stare at her trembling mouth. She watched his lips descend until they touched her own and her lids fell to shut out the light. Her hands went round his neck and clung, her lips opened and returned his kiss hungrily.

Ben held her close, his cheek against her hair. 'It will work,' he whispered. 'I'll make it work. We'll get married and live in the States, Joanne. There's bound to be some fuss in the press over it, but if we have a quick, discreet wedding we can be away before they find out, and once we're in the States I'll see to it that they don't get within an inch of you.'

'It isn't just the press,' she said miserably.

'Clea?' he asked brusquely, and she nodded.

'Forget her,' he said. 'We have our own lives to lead.' He tightened his arms around her, kissing her hair. 'I need you, Joanne. I'm incomplete without you.'

'Wait until your father is better,' she said. 'I can't rush into it, Ben. I need time to think.' She slid out of his arms and walked out of the room and he did not follow her.

She moved into the apartment with Clea and Milly, sharing the task of keeping Clea cheerful. The press were baying at the doors like wolves and for once Clea did not want to see them. She was obsessed with the idea that she was responsible for Jeb's illness. She was guilty, and like a child the guilt came out in little spurts of crying temper which Joanne had to smooth somehow.

Jeb recovered very slowly. He lay in his neat, white hospital bed, never moving, but his dark eyes recovered their life as day followed day. Clea was never allowed to see him alone. They all kept her from him because of her melancholy moods, and if she did go, Joanne went too. Jeb made no comment on that. Joanne suspected he understood only too well; he knew Clea. The violet eyes filled with tears at times. Jeb would look at her gently, shrewdly, and Joanne would quickly guide her from the room before she could upset him. For the moment they were more concerned with Jeb than Clea, his health was of paramount importance.

At last the doctors said he could go away to convalesce. Clea chose Nice, her favourite place. Jeb said he looked forward to seeing the villa again. 'A few weeks in the sun—that's just what I need.' He smiled at Clea. 'What we all need.'

Joanne did not want to go with them. As she saw it, her part of the job was done. Jeb was past the danger period. Clea was more cheerful. 'You can cope with her now,' she told Milly. 'I don't feel like staying at the villa.'

Milly eyed her regretfully. 'I wish you'd come, darling. You need a holiday yourself. You're looking grey.'

'I'm fine,' Joanne lied.

She and Ben had met from time to time, casually, politely, but she had made certain she was never alone with him again, and she suspected he would turn up at the villa if she was there.

'I must get another job,' she said. 'I have a living to earn.'

Clea was vociferous in her objections. 'You don't need to work. If you must do something, Milly could do with some help.'

Joanne smoothed her down carefully. 'I like living in London,' she said. 'I enjoy it. Nice is too quiet for me.'

'Quiet?' Clea was dumbfounded. 'Darling, you're kidding!'

They all flew off a few days later and Joanne saw them off at the airport, smiling brightly for the snapping photographers, her mood one of grey depression underneath.

She loved Ben, but she could not see that they had

any chance of happiness together. The past would always lie between them. Their parents had long ago wrecked any chance they might have had. How could Ben ever forget that her mother had helped to destroy his? Sooner or later he would remember that and he might come to hate her.

CHAPTER NINE

THE morning after they had gone, Joanne sat at a leisurely breakfast in her negligee, reading the papers and trying to decide what to do with her future. She could go back to the hotel, but she felt the time had come to make another break. Her father was furious with her for jilting Ralph. 'Your best chance,' he had called Ralph, and he had added that David and Patricia were insulted that she had behaved so callously to Ralph. Joanne had felt guilty and secretly rather hysterical as she listened to him. She could not tell her father that Ralph didn't give a damn for her; he would not have believed her.

The doorbell went and she opened the door to stare in surprise at a very small boy in a brown uniform who was struggling manfully under the weight of an enormous shell-shaped basket of red roses. 'Miss Ross?' he puffed, depositing them with a groan of relief.

When she had stood them in a corner of the sitting-room she plucked the card from where it had been cellotaped to the handle and read it with a smile. She sat down with her cup of coffee and stared at the flowers dreamily. Dark red, their petals smooth and fragrant, they had the beauty of total luxury. Ben had been ridiculously extravagant, but she was enchanted.

The doorbell went again ten minutes later. This time, she suspected, it would be Ben himself, and she hesitated before answering it, trying to marshal her arguments, to steel herself against him.

It was not Ben. It was the same boy with a second basket of red roses, this time arranged in a tapering fan, with silver fern backing them. Joanne laughed and the boy winked, putting them down. She gave him a tip and he pocketed it smoothly before trotting off.

The card held the same three words and she laid it on the table next to the first one, looking at them both with a torn expression on her face.

The boy was back a quarter of an hour later. This time as Joanne opened the door he groaned breathlessly, 'Hurry up and marry him, lady. It's killing me!'

She stood in the room glancing from one basket to another with rueful eyes.

Ben arrived five minutes later. When she opened the door he was leaning there, a red rose in his hand, and the dark eyes mocked her as she looked at him. 'Can I come in?'

'If you can get in,' she said. 'Some maniac has nearly drowned me in red roses. Be careful you don't knock any of them over.'

He wove the rose into her loose hair and smiled into her eyes. 'You got my message, then?'

'Indelibly,' she said.

'Have you ever read Browning's poems?' he asked,

pulling her long black hair across her throat with an air of concentration.

'Not that I recall.'

'He once wrote about a man who killed his mistress by winding her long hair round and round her throat,' he said, studying the effect of the black strands against her skin with apparent pleasure.

'Is that what you have in mind for me?'

The dark eyes flicked mockingly to her face. 'In the last resort,' he said. 'If you refuse to listen to the alternatives.'

She laughed. 'You seem fascinated by my hair.'

'Enthralled,' he said softly. 'For five years I've been dreaming of winding it through my hands while I make love to you, and I'm growing more and more impatient to fulfil my dreams.'

She felt her skin colouring and groaned. 'Ben, be sensible!'

'No,' he said. 'Let other people be sensible. We'll just be happy.'

'But could we be? I don't think it's possible for us.'

'We'll make it possible.'

'Clea...'

'Damn Clea,' he said. 'Forget she ever existed. There's just us, Joanne. We've neither of us had a very happy childhood, have we? At least let's make sure the rest of our lives are happy. I know I shan't be happy without you. What about you?'

She looked at him and knew that without him life would be empty for her. A sigh wrenched at her. 'Oh, Ben!'

He leaned his face against the side of her throat, his

mouth softly pushing aside the black strands still clinging to it. 'I love you,' he whispered against the warm
skin. 'Risk it, Joanne. Shut your eyes and jump into the
dark with me.'

'Let me think,' she muttered, but Ben had no intention of letting her think. One hand pushed aside her
negligee and she felt his fingers touching her breast,
his warmth reaching through the thin silk of her nightdress. His breathing quickened. 'No, Ben,' she whispered. He brushed his mouth against her bare shoulders
and his hand slid beneath the lace frill neckline of
the nightie. She gasped protestingly, but he could feel
the hardening of the nipple beneath his fingers and he
smiled down at her, the dark eyes teasing.

'You want me as much as I want you. I suppose I
knew that when I kissed you in Lester's garden that
first time. You looked so cool and sure of yourself, but
when you were in my arms you responded like a woman
in love. I wouldn't let myself believe it then, but afterwards I asked myself if you could have cared for me.
Once I'd admitted to myself that I cared for you I began to hope my suspicion had been right.'

She looked at him weakly, her body leaping with
response to the tantalising movements of his hands.
'Oh, Ben!'

'Darling,' he muttered.

They moved at the same moment, their mouths
meeting with a mutual flame which burnt higher and
higher as Joanne shed the last of her doubts and inhibitions, winding her arms around him, kissing him
wildly.

'I thought I might have damaged you beyond recovery,' Ben said to her later, smiling down at her as she lay cradled in his arms on the sofa. 'I behaved like a swine to you on that yacht. I was afraid I'd killed whatever you did feel for me.'

'Dented it,' she said wryly.

He stroked her face lovingly. 'And now?'

She made a face at him. 'I'm nuts about you and you know it.'

'I hoped it,' he said, his dark eyes full of warmth. 'I've got a marriage licence in my pocket. We'll get married on Wednesday morning and fly to the States straight away. We can cable the news from there.'

Joanne shook her head. 'I'm not taking a coward's way out, Ben. Either we face Clea with it or we don't do it at all.'

His face sobered. 'She might make trouble.'

'I don't care any more,' she said. 'I love you and I'm going to marry you.'

'You want to tell them first?' he asked doubtfully, his brows drawn together in a frown.

'No,' she said. 'We'll tell them afterwards, but we'll tell them to their faces.'

They looked like holidaymakers as they boarded a flight for Italy the following Wednesday. They had married so quietly that the press had not caught a hint of it. Before taking the plane they sent Clea and Jeb a brief cable. Married, it said. Love. Ben and Joanne.

They giggled over it as they made out the form and the clerk eyed them curiously. When she read the form she beamed at them.

'Congratulations,' she said, and they smiled back and left the post office hand in hand.

They spent their wedding night in Venice; Ben insisted on it. Their hotel was enormous, ramshackle and magnificent. Once a palazzo, it had a maze of marble corridors and great public rooms. Their suite looked out over the dark silk waters of the canal outside. Their bedroom led out on to a stone-balustraded balcony. 'I even ordered a crescent moon,' Ben said as they leaned on the ledge staring out over the city.

'Very efficient,' murmured Joanne, kissing his ear.

'Costly, though,' he said. 'God has a high price.'

She laughed, but her laughter died as he turned those dark eyes on her and the expression in them caught her breath in her throat.

Jerkily she walked back into the bedroom and picked up the glass of champagne she had been drinking with the supper they had eaten in the suite. Ben watched her, his face unreadable. When he walked to the bed she looked at him with a flushed, nervous face.

He sat down and gave her a long, thoughtful look. 'It may be an absurdly optimistic question, my darling, but will it still be the first time for you? I remember when you told me so five years ago, I was amazed ... moving in Clea's circle you could have led a pretty hectic love life.'

She was shaking and she couldn't stop. 'Watching Clea gave me the fixed impression that love wasn't all it was cracked up to be,' she said, trying to sound light-hearted.

'So I am the first,' he said, and she could read nothing in his voice, neither pleasure nor relief.

'Sorry if that disappoints you,' she said in brittle

tones. 'I realise you were expecting rather more experience.'

'Is that why you're clinging to that glass as if it were a rock?' he asked softly. 'Are you scared stiff, Joanne?'

She looked down, biting her lip.

Ben got up and she tensed, shooting him a nervous look. He lifted her into his arms as if she were a child and carried her to the bed. She shut her eyes and he kissed her very gently as he put her down. The light went out and panic lit in her like a beacon.

'Ben, I ...'

'Ssh!' he whispered, kissing her throat. She tried to tell him she wasn't ready, to beg him to stop, but her throat seemed to have lost the power to utter a word. His lips were moving over her, his hands travelling before them, shedding her clothes deftly as they went, discovering the warm flesh beneath with leisurely caresses.

Her hand lifted like that of a puppet, jerkily, as though someone else pulled the strings which controlled it. She touched his hair and he turned his cheek against her with a smothered groan.

His mouth found her own, their bodies softly moving, brushing against one another, the smooth warm contact of skin on skin, and she could hear her heartbeat racing. The panic of a moment ago was forgotten. She was burning in the heat he was engendering in her. The long, experienced hands touched her body slowly, delicately; transmuting her body from flesh to pure sensation. She was beyond the body, crying for fulfilment, and Ben gave it and took it from her in his turn.

'I love you,' she cried, shaken to her depths, and he groaned the words back, trembling against her body, above her, within her, engulfing her and engulfed.

Later the dark room was silent around them. 'That's how it is with us,' he said, his voice a shivering whisper. 'We couldn't throw that away.'

'Oh, no,' she groaned, and the thought of never having known such pleasure made her wince in horror.

His hard cheek was pressed into the yielding softness of her breast. 'And there's more to it than that.'

'Could there be?' she asked, laughing, yet catching her breath.

'Give me a lifetime and I'll prove it to you,' he said, and his head lifted from her body and she saw the dark eyes glittering in the arrogant face.

They fell asleep in each other's arms and woke in a cool Venetian sunrise to turn and smile at each other, still entwined. 'I feel free for the first time in my life,' said Ben. 'I feel as if I'm walking on air.'

'Funny,' she said. 'So do I. Can it be something catching?'

'I'm sure it is,' Ben said solemnly. 'I suggest we put a cross on the door and shut ourselves in here for weeks until we're sure we're not contagious.'

'Won't that be rather dull?' she asked, wide-eyed, and he bit her neck in mock-annoyance.

They spent two weeks in Italy, lazily wandering around, from city to city, in a hired car which had a peculiar habit of coughing to a halt on mountain roads and having to be started again by turning it downhill again. Even this bizarre practice amused them. They had shed years, returning for a while to adolescence.

Ben bought Joanne a pink marble mouse in a green marble hat and she adored it, useless though it was, giving it pride of place on her dressing-table. One day they bought a packet of balloons and spent an hour blowing them up. As they drove over a mountain road they released them one by one to float brilliantly through the pine trees fringing the mountainside and surprise the villagers below. Red, blue, yellow, they drifted down in the blue sky. A weather-lined man in a cart full of straw caskets stared at them as they let a balloon fly away. Joanne saw his sombre dark eyes gazing impassively, then he smiled, a sweet, warm smile, and they smiled back. 'Grazie,' he called, as though they had given the whole world a present, and they called back, 'Ciao!'

Joanne found herself waking up earlier and earlier, as though resenting the loss of even five minutes of time when she could spend it with Ben. They saw beauty everywhere, from the heavy black magnificence of the Medici chapels in Florence to the icecream smeared on a child's nose in a hilltop village. Life had opened its doors to them and they ran inside like ecstatic children.

'I didn't feel as young as this when I was five,' Ben said.

'Or as old,' said Joanne. 'I'm as old as these mountains.'

'We're yo-yos,' Ben agreed. 'To and fro in time ... my brain is totally disorientated. I may never return to earth.'

'Who wants to?' she asked, weaving a pigeon's feather into his tumbled hair.

But they had to, sooner or later, and they knew it.

Some time they had to go back to their world, face Jeb and Clea, and although Joanne felt no fear or jealousy of her mother now, she did not look forward to seeing her. She was not sure how Clea would take their marriage. She was not sure whether the resultant publicity which the marriage might stir would be a bitter experience for them all. The press might drag it up again, all that painful, ridiculous mess.

Their last night came too fast. They barely slept, clinging together like lost children, and she knew Ben feared the return as much as she did. They knew they loved each other, but they did not yet know how their love would stand up to the punishment it would take when they faced the rest of the world. The strain of public curiosity might tear them apart.

Their lovemaking had a frenzied quality, hectic and desperate. 'Love me,' Ben muttered, his hands hurting her. 'Love me, darling.'

'I do,' she whispered. 'I will ... always.'

'Always ...' The word seemed to catch in his throat. 'Whatever happens? Whatever ... anyone ... does or says?'

And then Joanne knew, as though he was telling her verbally, that he too feared Clea's intervention, her jealous anger, her vengeance.

Clea had dominated her life and Joanne still loved her, but she loved Ben far more and she would not allow her mother to come between them. She rocked him on her breast, her fingers stroking his hair. 'It will be all right,' she promised.

They flew to Nice and found Milly alone at the villa.

'They're in Nice,' she said, after she had kissed them and cried a little over Joanne.

Ben left Joanne alone with her discreetly and Milly asked her, 'Everything okay?'

Joanne understood the hidden question and smiled at her. 'Okay now and for ever,' she said. 'Clea okay?'

They were using verbal shorthand but understanding each other perfectly. 'Your cable announcing the marriage came as a shock to her,' Milly said, meeting her eyes.

Joanne paled. 'Oh!'

'Jeb was delighted, though,' Milly added. 'He looked as if his last hope had come in first.'

'I'm glad someone is on our side,' said Joanne.

'I am too,' Milly said protestingly.

'Thank you,' smiled Joanne, hugging her. She glanced at Milly and decided to tell her a piece of news she had kept from Ben. It was burning a hole in her mind and she had to tell someone. She had never taken any precautions against getting pregnant quite deliberately, and now it looked as though she might be going to have a child. She hoped desperately that she was, and although she and Ben had not yet discussed having children she was sure he wanted them.

'Clea will get over it,' Milly said later. 'Give her time.'

'I think I'm going to give her a grandchild,' Joanne said.

Milly's brows flew up. 'What?' Unspoken was the thought that they had only been married for two weeks, and Joanne laughed.

'Of course, I won't know for sure for weeks, but it is on the cards.'

Milly whistled. 'You wasted no time!'

'I've none to waste.'

'For yourself, or for Ben?' asked Milly drily.

Joanne's colour rose. 'I didn't get pregnant to hold him, if that's what you mean ... it just happened like that.'

'What does Ben feel?'

Joanne dimpled. 'I haven't told him.'

Milly's face flushed deeply. 'I'm the first to know?'

Joanne smiled at her. 'You're the mother I never had. Yes, you're the first to know. Are you pleased?'

Milly caught her breath, laughing and half crying. 'I'm sick with excitement! I couldn't be more pleased if it was my own.'

'It is, in a way, as I was your child, more yours than Clea's all my life.'

'When will you tell Ben?' Milly was finding the conversation too moving. She wanted to get on to more stable ground.

'When I'm sure,' said Joanne.

Ben came back and they smiled at him. He eyed them teasingly. 'What are you two up to? Secrets from me already?'

'We're planning your downfall,' Joanne said, and Milly laughed.

'So we are,' she said.

When Jeb and Clea came back they were laughing, but the laughter died as they saw who was waiting for them. Jeb flashed a look at Clea, and she stared at

Joanne with a stony face, her eyes almost black with hostility.

It was going to be even harder than she had supposed, and Joanne was shaken by that look.

'You sly creatures,' Jeb said very loudly, smiling far too much. 'Imagine keeping it a secret even from us! We ought to be very cross with you, but we're far too happy for you.'

He was making all this noise to cover Clea's fury and they helped him, laughing and talking, describing their honeymoon, rhapsodising about the Italian mountains, the sunsets and sunrises, the views of the green valleys, the rough Italian wine drunk in tiny villages.

Clea stood there, clenched and silent, and her eyes hated them both.

Joanne felt sick. Jeb tried to take Ben to look at some changes he had made in the gardens, but Ben would not leave her alone with Clea; he was terrified of what Clea would say or do, of the damage she could cause to them.

'Go and see them,' said Joanne, turning her eyes on him, willing him to go. She had to face her mother sooner or later and it might as well be now.

Ben was reluctant, and Jeb had to drag him away. When he had gone, Milly hovered, and Joanne gave her a quick, imploring look, but Milly would not go. She, too, was afraid of what Clea intended.

Clea turned on her suddenly. 'Get out,' she said in a rough, hoarse voice which was not recognisable as her own.

Milly tried to protest and Clea repeated it, even more hoarsely. 'Get out!'

Milly went, moving with dignity, her head held up, her face empty. Joanne waited, looking at Clea.

'Why him?' Clea asked in a shaking voice. 'You did it deliberately, took him away from me ... how did you get him to marry you? Let him seduce you and get pregnant? That's the usual trick, isn't it? You wanted him to pay me off, didn't you? You knew how he cared for me, you know it was me he wanted...'

It poured out like molten lava, boiling out of her mouth, and Joanne stared at her in silence, letting it wash over her, internally wincing at the burning sting of some of the words. On and on Clea ranted, her voice high-pitched, unbalanced. After a while she was repeating herself, the same phrases again and again, without stopping. Joanne made no attempt to answer or protest, she just listened and felt a terrible pity for her mother.

The tears began at last and they were a relief. Clea's eyes were burning and Joanne could see that there were tears behind them long before they fell, slowly at first and then a torrent.

She held her and stroked her hair and Clea, unbelievably, clung to her, weeping on her shoulder.

'I'm sorry, I'm sorry,' she choked like a bad child.

'It doesn't matter,' Joanne said. 'Ssh! Never mind...'

Jeb came in and sized up the situation at a glance. He took Clea out of her arms, holding her against him. Ben's in the garden,' he shaped silently with his mouth.

Joanne hesitated and he jerked his head.

She went out and joined Ben on the lawn. He looked at her anxiously. 'It's all right,' she said, hoping she was right, hoping that Clea had let the poison out of her system once and for all.

Clea did not appear again that day. Milly was absent, too, looking after her. 'A migraine,' Jeb said, and they pretended to believe it.

As Joanne walked with Jeb after dinner in the moonlight, he said to her, 'She'll get over it. It was another shock on top of a lot of others. Clea's having a bad time coming to grips with her age, and my illness didn't make it any easier for her. Then your marriage ... she feels old and she's frightened. Give her time, Joanne.'

'I will,' she promised.

In bed with Ben that night she sighed, 'Why is life so complicated? How much easier it is for birds!'

'Birds?' he laughed.

'They just get the urge and build a nest,' she said, and he laughed again.

'Where shall we build ours? It will have to be the States, you know. Somewhere within reach of New York.'

'And soon,' she said casually. 'We'll have around eight months.'

He didn't leap to it at once. 'Eight months? Why eight m ...' His voice stopped. 'Joanne?'

'I can't be certain,' she said nervously, shyly.

'God!' he muttered under his breath, and for one stricken moment she thought he was horrified, then she let out her breath with relief as he gave a deep sigh. 'God, Joanne, I hope it is.'

They hadn't talked about it. Now they did. 'You want children?'

'A family,' he said. 'Ours.'

'Yes,' she said, because with their mutual childhoods they knew the value of a family, of a home, of real, warm sharing. 'Ours.'

They lay cuddled up together, their bodies warm and silken after love, their voices hushed, talking about the hope of a baby, then he said, 'Clea is going to hate it.'

She shivered. 'I hope not.'

'My darling, face it, she will . . . being a grandmother would be bad enough, but our child . . .'

He did not need to say more, she knew just what he meant. Clea was jealous because Joanne had married Ben and he had once been one of the worshippers at Clea's shrine. He had deserted Clea, in her eyes, he had left when her beauty left, and she was bitter and resentful. Any child he gave Joanne would be a visible sign of that love which Clea fought against recognising, just as Joanne had once been a visible sign of Clea's age, hidden whenever possible, and her real age concealed when she was allowed to appear in public.

It was too complicated, too difficult. 'Let's go to America soon,' said Joanne.

'As soon as decently possible,' Ben promised.

They left a week later. Clea saw Joanne alone for a few moments and tried to be brave, Joanne could see her being brave and it was pathetic, she could almost hear Jeb warning her : be brave, my darling.

Her upper lip quivering, Clea smiled at her. 'I want you to be happy, darling. I really do . . . if he's the right man for you, I'm glad.' Her tone indicated deep uncertainty. 'He isn't an easy man.'

Joanne kissed her. 'We'll be fine, Clea.' She did not

mention the possibility of a baby, although it was becoming more and more a probability as day followed day.

Sufficient unto the day, she thought wryly. She rewarded Clea for her mask of sweetness. 'You look stunning in that new dress, don't let Lester see you in it—he's still pining, poor soul.'

Clea laughed, eyes sparkling. 'Isn't he? Such a sweet man, Lester. He's never married, you know.'

'Still hoping, I'm afraid, and all in vain.'

Clea loved to hear of men pining and hoping. She lit up like a Christmas tree. 'I'll miss you so when you're in the States.'

'You'll come and visit us.' But not too often, Joanne thought. No, Clea, not too often, and Jeb and I will see to that. Like most families, they loved each other best apart.

Ben had told Jeb about the hope of a baby. Jeb kissed her, taking her apart, whispering, 'I'm keeping my fingers crossed. I can't wait to be a grandfather!'

'Don't tell Clea,' she warned.

He gave her a wry look. 'Do you think I'm a fool? Only when I have to, believe me.'

Clea cried as she waved goodbye, and so did Milly, and of the two of them it was Milly whose tears were most real, and it was Milly for whom Joanne's answering tears fell. 'I'll miss her,' she said. 'More now than ever.' It would have been wonderful to take Milly with her, to lean on her strength while she waited for the baby, but she knew who needed Milly most and it was not her. 'I can cope, though,' she said aloud, and it was not just a calm remark, it was a shout of triumph, because for the first time in her life it was true and joyful.

'Of course you can,' said Ben, smiling. 'Even with me, brute though I am at times. Don't worry, I told Milly I would do all the cherishing needed.'

'Cotton wool?' she asked, tongue in cheek.

'I'll mummify you,' he teased, and they both laughed.

Joanne looked down from the plane and it was not just Clea and Milly she said goodbye to, but a long, bitter illness from which she had at last emerged. All her life she had been in Clea's shadow. She had resented, feared, envied, loved, admired her, and for the past five years all those emotions had churned inside her, making her sick, darkening the sky, ruining her life. Now she had Ben and that meant she had everything. She bore his child within her, she had his hand in her own. Down on the ground Clea had lost so much and Joanne found she could pity and love her again. She had regained her self-respect when she got Ben. She was no longer the girl nobody wanted. She was Joanne Norris, Ben's wife, and the whole world was her oyster.

Take these

4 best-selling novels
FREE

That's right! FOUR first-rate Harlequin romance novels by four world renowned authors, FREE, as your introduction to the Harlequin Presents Subscription Plan. Be swept along by these FOUR exciting, poignant and sophisticated novels . . . . Travel to the Mediterranean island of Cyprus in **Anne Hampson**'s "Gates of Steel" . . . to Portugal for **Anne Mather**'s "Sweet Revenge" . . . to France and **Violet Winspear**'s "Devil in a Silver Room" . . . and the sprawling state of Texas for **Janet Dailey**'s "No Quarter Asked."

The very finest in romantic fiction

Join the millions of avid Harlequin readers all over the world who delight in the magic of a really exciting novel. SIX great NEW titles published EACH MONTH! Each month you will get to know exciting, interesting, true-to-life people . . . . You'll be swept to distant lands you've dreamed of visiting . . . . Intrigue, adventure, romance, and the destiny of many lives will thrill you through each Harlequin Presents novel.

Get all the latest books before they're sold out!

As a Harlequin subscriber you actually receive your personal copies of the latest Presents novels immediately after they come off the press, so you're sure of getting all 6 each month.

Cancel your subscription whenever you wish!

You don't have to buy any minimum number of books. Whenever you decide to stop your subscription just let us know and we'll cancel all further shipments.